SPREAD ME

ALSO BY
SARAH GAILEY

Just Like Home

The Echo Wife

Magic for Liars

American Hippo: River of Teeth, Taste of Marrow, and New Stories

Upright Women Wanted

When We Were Magic

SARAH GAILEY

SPREAD ME

NIGHTFIRE
TOR PUBLISHING GROUP
NEW YORK

This is a work of fiction. All of the characters, organizations, and events portrayed in this novel are either products of the author's imagination or are used fictitiously.

SPREAD ME

Copyright © 2025 by Sarah Gailey

All rights reserved.

A Nightfire Book
Published by Tom Doherty Associates / Tor Publishing Group
120 Broadway
New York, NY 10271

www.torpublishinggroup.com

Nightfire™ is a trademark of Macmillan Publishing Group, LLC.

EU Representative: Macmillan Publishers Ireland Ltd, 1st Floor, The Liffey Trust Centre, 117–126 Sheriff Street Upper, Dublin 1, DO1 YC43

The Library of Congress Cataloging-in-Publication Data is available upon request.

ISBN 978-1-250-38733-2 (hardcover)
ISBN 978-1-250-38734-9 (ebook)

The publisher of this book does not authorize the use or reproduction of any part of this book in any manner for the purpose of training artificial intelligence technologies or systems. The publisher of this book expressly reserves this book from the Text and Data Mining exception in accordance with Article 4(3) of the European Union Digital Single Market Directive 2019/790.

Our books may be purchased in bulk for specialty retail/wholesale, literacy, corporate/premium, educational, and subscription box use. Please contact MacmillanSpecialMarkets@macmillan.com.

First Edition: 2025

Printed in the United States of America

10 9 8 7 6 5 4 3 2 1

For
everyone
who thinks
loneliness
is
inevitable

SPREAD ME

The specimen is breathing.

Kinsey is the first to see it.

Most of the people on her team are looking at the horizon, where a dust-brown stripe has been growing thicker over the course of the past hour. A sandstorm is on the way. Kinsey's been peering at it intermittently through her binoculars, trying to figure out how fast it's moving. How much time they have to study the creature they found buried in the sand before it gets buried again beneath a layer of windblown dust.

She's the one who makes the call: the storm is moving too quickly to risk staying out here to study the creature. Even without returning to the research station so Domino can consult Weatherman, she can tell. It's time to bring the specimen inside. That brown belt between the ground and the sky is growing fast, gaining height as it draws closer with every passing second, and it's making her nervous. She's nervous and her team can tell that she's nervous and her being nervous makes all of them nervous, because it takes a lot to make Kinsey nervous. And it doesn't pay to be nervous in the desert. So she's got to get them inside.

The team stumbles as they move across the sand toward the research station, trying to keep their eyes on the hell that's coming for them. And because their eyes are on the horizon, Kinsey is the only one watching when the specimen draws breath.

She doesn't tell anyone on the team at first. If she tells them, shock will loosen at least one pair of hands, and then they'll all drop the shitty tarp they're using to haul the specimen inside. They're already struggling to keep a grip on the weathered plastic, their sweat-slick hands slipping, their knuckles white, their thick-soled, dust-caked boots sliding across the sand. She doesn't want them distracted, so she doesn't offer explanations; when they get to the base, she just slams her elbow against the big red button next to the exterior intercom.

"Mads, come let us in. I need an exam table. Now."

The answer is immediate. "Did you forget your keycard again? Why aren't you calling on your walkie?"

"Hands are full. We need help. Make it quick, there's a storm coming."

"On my way."

Domino reacts first, which isn't unusual. Domino is always the first to notice things, quick to speak up. They were the first to bring up the possibility of the storm today, when they spotted the incoming data on Weatherman.

SPREAD ME

When Kinsey mentions the storm, Domino's eyes meet hers, and the space between their brows slams shut.

Domino is gripping two fistfuls of tarp at the far end of the specimen. They're wearing a faded pink crop top with the words *Baby Slut* emblazoned across the chest. It's threadbare, damp with sweat, riddled with holes that will leave cheetah-spots of deep tan across Domino's shoulders. Kinsey has tried to forbid this shirt at least twenty times, a dress code edict that Domino always insists "doesn't count." Now, as they contort their neck to wipe their dripping forehead on the cutoff sleeve, their expression is one of naked confusion. "Boss? We should have another hour or so before the storm really—"

Kinsey shakes her head. "We'll talk about it when we're full-in," she snaps, meaning *don't ask me any more questions until we're past the airlock.*

She doesn't like brushing off Domino's confusion, especially in a way that she knows will raise more questions. Normally, when the team finds something that needs to come inside for further study, they carry whatever they've found into the airlock and stop there. That's where they decide their next steps, assign tasks and catalog observations, comb through all the little tangles of detail that feel impossible when they're standing outside under the relentless eye of the desert sun.

That order of operations is less feasible with a sandstorm on the way. The airlock is too exposed to the freight-train howl of the wind and the lashes of driving sand that will hit the base. And even if there wasn't a storm coming, procedure stopped mattering once Kinsey saw the specimen's lips part. Once she saw the sand fall onto its tongue. Once she saw it choke on a tiny, silent cough.

Seeing that should have made her tell her team to drop the tarp. *Living things don't get brought inside*—that's the rule she's ignoring, and soon, her team will know she ignored it. They'll want to know why.

She doesn't know how to explain it to them. She can't explain it to herself, either.

There's the beep of a card reader near Kinsey's left shoulder and then the door behind her swings open. The doorframe immediately fills with the towering rectangle that is Mads. "Exam table, huh? We got an injury? Jacques, I told you to drink water today."

"It's not for me," Jacques objects.

"Who, then? Ah, shit, you weren't kidding about the storm coming in. I should have been checking Weatherman."

Kinsey can feel the solidity of Mads's body coming close to hers. They get that way when there's an emergency, losing their typical strict regard for personal space in the interest of attacking whatever problem has presented itself. Their chest presses flush against her back, their omnipresent stethoscope digging into her shoulder blade. Their chin brushes the crest of her ear as they try to peer around her at the horizon.

She feels their breath catch as they spot the specimen. "What in the—"

"Exam table," Kinsey repeats, barreling past Mads since they decided to be in her way. "Right now. Help or don't."

"What is that thing?" Mads yells as they jog to get ahead of her, their holey white sneakers crunching across the sandy linoleum. They pass the pegboard wall where the keys to the largely disused Jeep hang, then swing around the low IKEA shelves that hold everything the team discards on their way in and out of the station—jackets, flashlights, sunglasses, spare keycards, walkie-talkies in their charging stations.

The interior card reader beeps as Mads scans in, and then comes a soft sucking sound as they tug the interior door open. A gentle rush of air from within pushes Kinsey's hair into her face and sends ripples across the sand on the airlock floor.

Jacques, who never wears sunscreen and is hungover one hundred percent of the time, is the first to answer Mads's question. "Domino found it," he says, one corner of his mouth lifting with wry affection. It's impossible to see his eyes behind his mirror shades, but guaranteed he's casting an adoring glance at Domino. Those two have been fucking for about four months as far as Kinsey knows. Jacques is definitely in love. Domino is definitely not.

"Should have been helping me map the grid for tomorrow's samples. Not that there's much point since it'll be buried by the end of the day anyway," Nkrumah snaps, her tongue ring clicking against her front teeth on the *th*s. She's pissed about Domino and Jacques fucking. Kinsey isn't sure which of them is the target of Nkrumah's possessive jealousy. Could be both. "What were you doing digging, anyway?"

Domino replies without meeting Nkrumah's bid for conflict. "I had to piss."

"Who digs a hole just to piss?"

"Fine. I had to take a shit. I just didn't want to say so. You happy?"

"Go left," Kinsey says.

The team knows where they're going. Of course they do. But she doesn't want to have to listen to Nkrumah and Domino bickering. Especially knowing that they'll both come vent to her about it later—Domino frustrated,

Nkrumah heartbroken, both of them tired and dehydrated and pissed off.

She knows they'll vent about it to her because she's the person everyone vents to. That's the consequence of not participating in the lacelike web of hookups and breakups and romances and letdowns that develop in a situation like this one—she's treated as a neutral party. For months at a stretch, Kinsey's isolated six-person research team curls in on itself, touching itself and talking to itself and mutilating itself and eating itself, and—when it comes to the members of the team who *aren't* Kinsey—fucking itself. And complaining to her about all of it. Kinsey loves her team, but she sometimes thinks that managing them is like having a lab partner who won't stop talking about how they cry after jerking off.

Maybe it's just because she's hot and tired from cataloging lichens in the sun all day, and maybe it's because the storm is coming and coming fast—but right now, Kinsey doesn't want to deal with the seepage of their entanglements. Not when there's about to be something that looks like a six-legged multi-segmented coyote on a rat-gnawed tarp in the exam room.

She needs time to look at it more closely. To count the joints on those six legs. To figure out if there's a tapered wasplike waist or just a rotted belly sinking into the barrel of the ribcage. She can't memorize the feel of that patchy, coarse fur, not if she's dealing with her team and their endless, recursive drama. She needs space. She needs to be alone with the thing they've found.

She *needs* it.

"Boss," Domino says again. "Why are we taking this thing full-in? There's still time left before the storm hits us, we could just tag it and head back out."

"Load it," Kinsey says brusquely. It's the kind of nonanswer the team hates from her, the kind that supplies no information. Too bad.

She bumps into Mads, her shoulder against their elbow, her heel landing on their toes. They don't complain. They never complain. The door to the exam room is wedged open, a thick paperback crushed between door and doorframe. It's *Tropic of Cancer*—Mads swears it's unreadable, useful only as a doorstop, but every time Kinsey looks at it she notices more dog-ears among the pages. It flops to the floor as Mads uses a foot to push the door open wide enough to admit the team.

Saskia stops in the doorway, halting the team's progress just a few steps from the exam table. Desert sand rains down from the tarp as it pulls taut. Saskia is staring down at the specimen, her pale eyes enormous, her jaw slack. Kinsey wants to scream at her to move—they're so close to getting to put this thing down.

"What?" Kinsey snaps.

"It moved," Saskia whispers. The Eastern Orthodox cross around her neck has slipped loose of her mostly unbuttoned shirt. It's stuck fast to the sweat-tacky expanse of her décolletage, the angled crossbar drawing a cockeyed line between the swell of each of her breasts. "I swear to god it just—"

She doesn't get to finish her thought, because Jacques's grip on the tarp falters. The plastic slides out of his fists. The specimen rolls toward him. He lunges, hangover-clumsy, for the edge of the tarp—but he catches a fistful of the specimen instead. His hand finds one of the legs that emerge from the center of the specimen's abdomen, his fingers sinking into the surprisingly lush fur that covers the limb.

He lets go with a yell, and the specimen comes awake.

The barrel of its chest heaves as it chokes on sand and thick saliva. Its jaw slackens, three long tongues unbraiding, a stream of gritty mucus falling from the corners of its mouth. It lets out a sound like it's breathing through gravel.

Kinsey lets out a wordless cry. She tries to drag the team and the tarp backward with her, hauling them deeper into the exam room, aiming the many-legged mass of researchers toward the table.

Nkrumah, Jacques, and Saskia don't follow her. They bolt out of the exam room, slamming the door shut behind them. It's the right thing to do and they all should have done it. There's no protocol for a wild animal getting into the research station but if there was one, it would include the words *run away fast*. They're all smart enough to know that.

Still, not everyone runs. Mads grabs hold of the tarp. Along with Kinsey and Domino, they clench the plastic into a loose bundle around the thing as it writhes, swinging it toward the exam table hard enough that they're practically throwing it.

By some miracle it lands in the right place. It drops onto the exam table with all the heft of a waterlogged mattress. Mads and Domino each take an immediate step backward. The tarp is still folded loosely over the specimen, the plastic rising and falling fast as the creature pants beneath it.

It's scared, Kinsey thinks. She's breathing fast too.

The crinkling movement of the tarp is matched by a rhythmic sound that Kinsey only belatedly recognizes as the sound of Nkrumah tapping a finger against the thick glass of the exam room window. Nkrumah, bossy and brisk, always safety-minded. She'll want to call some kind of meeting about how Mads and Kinsey and Domino didn't leave the room. She'll want to agree on new rules, then print them out and laminate them and tape them to the exam room door.

1. When the monster we find beneath the desert sand turns out to be alive, we all get away from it.

A thick wet sound comes from beneath the tarp. Another choking cough. Nkrumah keeps tapping her finger on the glass, but Kinsey doesn't give a shit about Nkrumah right now. The entire research station falls away. It's just her and the specimen.

Kinsey steps toward it.

"Hey," Mads pants, their voice a million miles away. "Hey, maybe don't."

They're too late. Even if they weren't, Kinsey would act like they were. She reaches out one trembling hand and lifts the folded-over tarp off the specimen.

It twists its head. The long snout angles toward her. The damp dimpled nostrils flex as it searches for the smell of her. Kinsey doesn't move. She doesn't know what she's waiting for until the moment the specimen's eyelids snap open. There are no eyes in the sockets—only densely packed sand. Still, when it turns toward Kinsey she feels something impossible, something she never gets to feel anywhere else.

She feels *noticed*.

"Hi," she breathes.

The specimen lets out a low gurgle. A single red-and-black harvester ant wriggles free of the sand in the left eye socket, crawls down over the specimen's cheek, makes its way down one leg of the exam table.

"Boss," Domino says. At the sound of their voice, Kinsey feels the research station slam back into place around her. "Hey. Boss. We need to walk out of this room now, okay?"

Kinsey nods. "Yeah. Okay." She doesn't take her eyes off the specimen.

"Kinsey," Mads adds. "Now."

She doesn't make them drag her out of the room. She turns away on her own steam. As she opens the exam room door, she can feel the weight of the specimen's eyeless gaze on her back.

Once the exam room door is shut behind them, Mads lets out a shaky breath. "Holy shit."

"That thing's alive," Domino breathes. "How the hell is it alive?"

"Where did you find it again?"

"Like a hundred meters from the survey grid," Domino answers. "Under, I don't know, two feet of sand? I started digging and the ground just kind of collapsed under me, and—Boss? Are you okay?" They might as well be on the other side of the world, talking to Kinsey through a tin can. "She doesn't look okay."

Kinsey doesn't answer. She brushes at a tickle on her neck and feels something small and damp roll beneath the weight of her touch. She catches it between her fingers and when she brings her hand in front of her face, she realizes that she's holding the half-mangled body of a harvester ant. Maybe the same one that came out of the specimen's eye socket, maybe not—there are always ants around the station. Its antennae wave slowly, tasting her breath on the air.

Kinsey licks her lips, then tucks the ant into the pocket of her jeans.

"Team meeting," she says at last. "Now."

"I'm so glad you're here." Kinsey opens the passenger door of the Jeep for Nkrumah, but doesn't offer to help with either of the large duffel bags at her feet. In the four hours it took to drive from the airstrip to the research base, Kinsey came to understand one thing quite clearly: Nkrumah prefers to haul her own load.

"Glad to be here," Nkrumah replies. She scuffs her boots in the sand, getting the toecaps dusty. "That's better. Hate the look of a new boot."

Kinsey grins and pulls out two keycards. "Don't worry. It won't last long. This is for you," she adds, flashing one of the keycards before tucking it into the side pocket of one of the duffels. "You'll need it to get in and out of the airlock."

Nkrumah's chin tilts upward, her brows dropping. This is something Kinsey noticed during the interview process:

Nkrumah tends to ask questions with an air of authority. "Airlock?"

"Come see." She scans her own keycard against the pad on the outside of the exterior door, waiting for it to let out a beep before turning the handle. "This place was originally supposed to house astronauts-in-training. They were still building it when that budget massacre hit NASA. You remember the—?"

"Yes." The answer carries the weight of what it felt like to be a research scientist during that particular presidential administration. What it's felt like ever since.

They walk into the dim airlock. It's a narrow hallway, wider at the far end. It does a so-so job of keeping the outside out and the inside in. The floor is permanently blanketed with desert sand, the walls ornamented with the tiny pissed-off lizards that always manage to find their way in. Still, it's better than nothing, and it's good to have two locking doors between the lab and the intense indifference of the desert.

"Yeah, so. The base was originally supposed to be a circle. Kind of bicycle-wheel shaped, with a recreation area in the middle where that cement pad out front is now. This airlock system was put in place for the baby astronauts to practice secure entry and egress from each spoke of the wheel. But then funding got vaporized, and they had to abandon construction partway in."

"Ah." Nkrumah looks around, taking in the near-triangular dimensions of the airlock. "They just connected the spokes? So we have a . . . pie slice?"

"Got it in one. Twenty-five hundred square feet, tons of dead space between hallways," Kinsey adds, crossing the airlock to scan her keycard at the interior door. "It's not a lot of breathing room for six people, but we'll make it work."

SPREAD ME

"I've lived in smaller apartments with more roommates."

Kinsey hesitates at the door. "I'd wager those apartments had reliable cell service and Wi-Fi. Ours gets knocked out by dust storms half the time. Hell, in the bad sandstorms even the emergency landline goes down, and repairs on that can take months. Phone company's not exactly prioritizing line repairs in the middle of nowhere."

The only sound for a moment is the creak of Nkrumah's new boots as she shifts her weight from foot to foot. "Are you trying to get me to turn around? Head back to the airstrip? Miss out on the opportunity to put Kangas Station on my resume?"

"No. No, sorry. I just—I want you to know what you're getting into here. That's all. Hope you're ready to get cozy with some strangers."

She looks back to see a wicked sparkle in Nkrumah's eyes. "Oh, I don't think that will be a problem." Her mouth slowly spreads into a Cheshire-cat grin. "The real question is—are *they* ready to get cozy with *me*?"

The keycard scanner beeps. Kinsey opens the door. "Let's find out."

The meeting starts with all the usual formalities. Nkrumah yells about safety protocols and asks Domino whether they are or are not "a fucking idiot"; Saskia asks Nkrumah not to swear; Nkrumah swears again, more pointedly this time. Mads asks everyone to calm down. Domino sits silently with their arms folded, their eyes half-shut, their mouth pressed into a tight line. Jacques vomits into a trash can.

Kinsey knows how these things go. It's all predictable, all self-contained. This part doesn't require her intervention. Nkrumah always snaps at whoever she feels most recently rejected by. Saskia latches on to everyone's tone, and acts wounded by all but the softest verbal caresses. Mads is infuriatingly, antagonistically reasonable. Domino seethes. Jacques vomits into a trash can.

She half listens to them, her forehead pressed to the

glass of the little window that looks into the exam room, her skin tacky with half-dried sweat. Her gaze is fixed on the wire mesh that's embedded in the glass. She wonders how they got it in there. Did the wire get sandwiched between two layers of glass, like a specimen being prepared for study? Or did the glass get poured over the wire, sealing it inside?

Either way, she wants that experience for herself. She wants to be the wire. Never corroding, never rusting, never plucked at by human fingers. A layer of glass between her and the world. Sealed away. That's what she loves about this tiny wedge of a building she lives in: the miles of isolation on all sides of it. This place affords her a way to keep everything, everyone, at a hundred arms' lengths.

Everyone except for her team, who drift around inside the research station like glitter in a snow globe, smacking into each other's bodies and feelings with seemingly no direction or thought at all.

Beyond the wire, beyond the glass, inside the exam room, the specimen isn't moving. Kinsey can't tell if it's still breathing. She wonders why she can't seem to stop licking her lips.

"Let's find out what the boss thinks." That's Domino, right on time, breaking their sullen silence to appeal to Kinsey's authority.

Kinsey turns to the team like a clockwork figurine that's just been wound up. "Nkrumah, quit yelling at everyone. Jacques, drink some water. Mads, either get shorter or sit down. Domino . . . can you go check Weatherman?"

"On it." Domino is already on their feet, headed down the hall toward the lab.

She lets her head fall back to rest against the glass, so she's staring down her nose at her team. They're sitting in the vestibule outside the exam room. It used to be dead space between spokes in the quarter-wheel of the station. The team knocked it out six months into their assignment, in a fit of ill-supervised restlessness. There's a small round table in there that wobbles constantly, two mismatched folding chairs, a faded love seat with duct-tape patches on the cushions. The team is crammed into that nook—some sitting, some standing, all irritated.

Kinsey's heart swells at the sight of them like a streambed in a flash flood. Their cheeks are flushed. Their eyes are bright. They're electrified, all of them, with the spark of discovery.

The specimen did this to them, Kinsey thinks. The specimen did this *for* them. Everything she's ever done—every blister that's ever bubbled up on her sun-cooked shoulders, every scorpion she's ever shaken out of her boot, every rule she's ever broken—it's all been worth it. For this. For them.

"Why is the specimen in here?" Saskia asks. She's chewing on her lip, jogging one knee fast enough to make the table vibrate. The zippers on the pockets of her cargo pants rattle. "We aren't even properly set up to examine it safely. All our PPE is inside the exam room with that fucking thing. We're functionally helpless. Why'd we bring it full-in? Why expose ourselves to all that risk?"

Kinsey can't even answer that question to herself, much less to Saskia. "What matters now is what we do with it," she says instead.

"We're not doing anything with it," Nkrumah insists.

"Oh no," Jacques groans, shortly before leaning over the trash can again.

Kinsey presses one hand to her forehead. "Everyone shut up," she says. "I need to think."

Nkrumah scoffs. "All due respect, your last thought gave us some kind of... fucking... *Thing* to deal with."

Every eye in the room turns to her. Kinsey points wordlessly at a jar on the little round table. There's a sticky note taped to the front of the jar with a ballpoint frowny face drawn on it. A slot has been cut in the plastic lid. About five hundred dollars in small bills sit inside.

Nkrumah holds her hands out defensively. "I didn't."

"You did," Mads says. "We all heard you."

"It's a completely neutral pronoun!"

Saskia shakes her head. "There was a capital letter on it. You know the rules. You reference the movie, you feed the jar."

Nkrumah heaves a theatrical sigh, then stands and crosses to the folding table. She pulls a crumpled, sweat-softened five-dollar bill from her bra and drops it in.

All the money inside will eventually go to Sweet Ramona, the proprietor of the only bar in Boot Hill, the closest thing to a town within a hundred miles. Every six months, the team piles into the Jeep and makes a pilgrimage to Sweet Ramona's Taphouse to get shithoused toasting their isolation. One by one, Kinsey asks each of them if they want to clock out. For each person who says no, she buys the team a round. After the fifth round, they all ask her if *she* wants to clock out. When she says no, they hand the jar to Ramona herself; she'll pour them a generous round of something off the dust-furred top shelf, they'll leave her whatever's left in the jar as an outrageously huge tip, and everyone will be hungover for three full days after.

Nkrumah doesn't contribute to the jar often, but it's impossible not to make John Carpenter references when you work at a research station in the middle of fucking nowhere. Fair's fair. Mads takes Nkrumah's seat while she's up.

At the far end of the hall, the lab door opens. Domino emerges, backlit by the red glow of Weatherman's display. They hold up two fists, their thumbs pointed down. "It's gonna be bad."

"How bad?" Jacques groans.

"Three days, minimum. This place is gonna be a dune by sunrise."

The entire team responds in unison, "Fuck you, Weatherman."

"It's just doing its job," Domino says loyally, even though they'd also cursed the satellite computer that keeps them all aware of incoming storm systems. "What'd I miss?"

"Well, first things first," Mads says. "What is that... animal?"

"A coyote," Jacques replies hoarsely.

"Coyotes don't have six legs," Domino replies. "And three tongues."

A gust of wind rattles the base, and everyone looks up, as if they'll be able to see the encroaching sandstorm through the ceiling. There's no point being vigilant about something as inevitable and unpredictable as a wall of sand hurtling across the desert. But they're all being vigilant anyway. They can't help it. They're just animals in a little box hoping to finish out the day without dying.

Kinsey keeps her eyes on the ceiling to prevent herself from looking through the exam room window again. "We don't know what the specimen is. But last time I checked, we're scientists. Figuring this kind of thing out is what we're here for," she says. "We'll document everything. Write a paper. Saskia and Nkrumah can do the conference circuit."

"Why do they get to do the conference circuit?" Mads grumbles.

Saskia aims a wink at Nkrumah. "Because we're a good team."

Jacques heaves into the trash can again.

"Fucking hell, Jacques." Kinsey tries to make her voice playful, but it doesn't work. "Can you get it together?"

"Sorry," he says into the depths of the trash can. "I don't feel s'good."

Mads frowns. "You're not usually still throwing up this late in the day." They look at him with what Kinsey thinks of as their doctor-face: watchful, assessing, a calculator made flesh. "J, anything else going on with you? Do you have sunstroke?"

"Don't think so?" Jacques looks up blearily. His lips are white. Crimson circles like vaudeville rouge stain his already-ruddy cheeks. His eyes shine with an unwholesome glassiness.

Kinsey stares at him, yearning flooding her belly. She presses her thighs together hard. *Stop it*, she tells herself. *Stop it stop it stop it*.

Mads stands abruptly. "Everybody out of this wing," they announce. "Now."

Nkrumah doesn't budge. "What? Why?"

"Jacques made unprotected contact with the specimen, and now he has a fever," Mads says.

"You can't know he has a fever just by looking."

"I can and I do. That"—Mads says, pointing decisively at Jacques—"is a fever. We have to quarantine until we know if whatever he's got is contagious. I'll treat him, but the rest of you have to go."

"But animal-to-human transmission is—"

"Not that rare, especially these days," Kinsey interrupts, her voice mortifyingly husky. She hopes they'll all think she's sick. "Saskia, I believe your second doctoral thesis . . . ?"

"Yes, that was my focus," Saskia says, her voice tight with restrained enthusiasm. Kinsey can tell she's holding herself back, trying not to get too excited about the opportunity to discuss her deep interest in the subject—and she doesn't entirely succeed at the effort. "Kinsey's right. Climate change has escalated the ability of viruses and fungal infections to achieve zoonotic spillover and—"

"Right," Kinsey cuts in. She knows she should let the team hear Saskia out, but she feels like she's going to climb out of her skin with impatience. "You all know the rules. The doc says the Q word, that's it. If Domino read Weatherman right—"

"I did."

"—then it sounds like that storm would keep us inside anyway. We're under quarantine until further notice. Use the time to, I don't know, meditate on the nature of lizards. Mads, you want me to run and grab you some gloves from the lab?"

Mads gives her a long look. They both know that Mads should be taking Jacques into the exam room, should be getting gloves and a mask from the drawers in there, should be leaving Jacques inside with a roll of duct tape so he can seal himself in with whatever illness is currently working its way through his system.

But they can't do any of that, because the specimen is in the exam room, and the specimen is alive.

Saskia sways on her feet. "Actually. Wow. I don't feel great, either. I feel . . . weird."

Mads releases Kinsey from the butterfly pin of their gaze. "'Weird' means sick. If you feel weird, go to your quarters. Isolate as much as you can. The rest of us, the name of the game is 'abundance of caution,' yeah? Those of us who aren't ill will drop food outside your doors every ten hours, but otherwise, we'll avoid the residential wing as much as possible. We'll sleep on the couches in the canteen tonight. We can use the lab bathroom." No one audibly groans at the prospect of using the strange, tiny toilet that sits behind a thin partition in the lab next to the eyewash station, but an aggrieved glance travels quickly around the room. Mads ignores it. "Maybe if we isolate, whatever this is will only hit some of us."

"Good plan," Kinsey says, trying not to talk too fast or seem too eager. "I feel a little strange too. I'm going to head to my bunk. Domino, keep an eye on Weatherman as long as you can, yeah? Also, we should probably burn that shirt just to be safe. Toss it in the biohazard bin when you get a chance?"

Domino flips her a good-natured middle finger. "Feel better, Boss."

She nods to them. "Good luck, team."

Everyone veers off. Kinsey slips into her room.

The room is plain. It's a solo berth she managed to claim by default. Even though she's the only one in the room, it still has twin beds on opposite walls, one of which she uses as a makeshift shelf for the dune of binders that accumulate around every poor fool who ends up managing a research team. Heavy blankets on both beds, two pillows on the one she sleeps in. No windows, no closet. There's a scratchy jute rug on the floor, a wobbly flat-pack dresser with a too-bright lamp on top, a framed poster with a wide-angle photo of a desert that isn't this one. One wall radiates heat during the day because it's got the desert on the other side of it. She can hear the wind picking up through that wall. It's getting more intense by the second—this storm is fast.

Her instincts were right, having everyone come inside. She's sure of it. She's less sure of her instincts about the specimen, but what's done is done.

The second the door closes behind her, Kinsey takes that framed poster of a distant desert off the wall. There's another, much smaller photo stuck to the back of the frame with paper lab tape. She peels the tape away carefully so as not to rip the paper on the back of the frame. It's not difficult—she's been removing and re-sticking this same photo for two months, and the tape's morale is low. She'll need to replace it soon, she knows.

But that doesn't matter right now.

She turns the photo over with unspeakable relief. She hasn't recovered from the first flush of desire, which hit her at a bizarre, inopportune moment—when the specimen opened its eyes, when it seemed to look at her. A mixed-up panic impulse, she figures. The kind of thing that happens all the time. Kinsey still remembers the neuropsych professor who taught her class the five F's of adrenaline response: *fight, flight, freeze, fawn, and procreate*. In the nervous system, that professor said, fear and arousal are always going steady.

Still, it was jarring to experience that sudden, strange, misplaced lust when the specimen awoke. It primed Kinsey's proverbial pump. It left her vulnerable. She's a strong person, but she's not made of stone. When Jacques looked up from his puke-filled trash can with such an obvious fever, when Saskia looked ready to faint, when Mads said the word *quarantine*—it was all too much.

Kinsey's decision to isolate herself in her bedroom isn't

because she feels ill. It's just that she's so horny she thinks she might die from it.

She collapses onto her bed with the photo in one hand. Her lower lip is between her teeth already, her eyes locked on the black-and-white image. It's a famous picture in certain circles. One of the finest examples of electron microscopy in the world.

A T2 bacteriophage.

The wind squeals against the walls of the station as Kinsey stares hungrily at the photo of the virus. The long, slim, spidery fibers it uses to quest for a host splay out at wanton angles. A thick, sturdy, rodlike sheath connects the fibers at one end of the bacteriophage to the capsid on the other, like a body connects legs to a head. The multifaceted capsid looks for all the world like the candy sphere of a lollipop.

It's perfect.

She drinks in the stretch of those fibers. The stunning geometry of the capsid. She imagines herself as an unsuspecting bacterium—the feel of the virus grasping her with its fibers, the sudden shock of penetration when it slides its sheath through her cell wall, the invasive rush of nucleic acid being injected into her. She thinks of what it would feel like when that genetic material started replicating inside of her, changing her, taking her over—the heat, the hum, the rising tide of infection.

This is all she wants. This is all she's ever wanted. The wind outside is howling now, a low air-raid drone. The wall of her room shivers as the first real gust of sand hits it.

She unbuttons her jeans and shoves them down around her thighs, her eyes locked onto the photo. The denim digs into the soft meat of her skin, keeps her from being able to spread her legs too far. She knows that this is how it would feel to be restrained by strong bacteriophage fibers. Transfixed. Unable to escape.

When she pushes her pinched thumb and forefinger inside of herself, she imagines them as belonging to something transformative, grotesque, peregrine. No lover has ever fingered her this way—she loves it because of how alien it feels, how inhuman. She bites her own shoulder to muffle a cry as she thinks of the virus shooting itself into her just like this. Careless. Invasive. Trying to make her into something more like itself. Changing her. Alien. Relentless. Irresistible.

She's close, so close, when she feels something strange—a tickle on her hipbone, like a trailing hair. She almost ignores it—she's right there—but then she glances down and sees it.

The harvester ant from the specimen.

She'd shoved it into her pocket, truly unthinking in that panicked moment, muscle memory guiding her hand. Now, it drags its half-crushed body across her skin. The ant's antennae wave drunkenly as it charts a path across her hipbone, toward the wet ache between her legs. The storm outside rises to a high scream.

Kinsey doesn't breathe. She relaxes her eyes, presses her thumb and forefinger together tighter inside herself, lets her vision blur—and the ant stops looking like an ant. The slender expanse of its thorax looks cylindrical for a moment, the questing node of its head looks gemlike, the now-useless legs it drags behind it take on the trailing elegance of bacteriophage fibers. It pulls itself across her flesh toward the shady refuge of her groin. Kinsey watches it with half-lidded eyes and fucks herself deeper, rougher, hard enough that the knuckle at the base of her thumb aches. She dips her chin so she can clench her teeth around a mouthful of shirt collar. She rides a cresting wave, the feel of the ant and her pulsing fingers and her own bucking hips turning her animal.

It rips through her like lightning. She bites back a cry, her wrist slamming down onto the soft mound of her pubis as she rises to meet the orgasm. The freight-train scream of the sandstorm striking the base covers the noise she can't make herself hold in. She's faintly aware of a pinpoint sensation beneath the skin of her inner arm—the ant, wriggling desperately. Trapped between her and her pleasure. She ignores it, thrusts against herself again and again, still coming, still coming, still coming.

The ant dies before she's finished. She falls asleep to the sound of the screaming sand bearing down on her, one hand still tucked between her legs, the other still clutching the photo of the bacteriophage.

By the time she wakes up, everyone on her team has entered isolation.

Kinsey eyes the new station physician with a combination of suspicion and preemptive resentment. She doesn't trust them. She doesn't like that they're here. She certainly doesn't like that they're here before any of her own hires.

"Who dropped you off?" she asks as she leads them through the interior airlock door.

"TQI sent a car," they reply, dropping their bags onto the linoleum just inside the station. "It was nice. There were little bottles of Cîroc in the back."

The mention of TQI makes Kinsey's tongue twitch against the roof of her mouth. They're a finger on the hand of one of the biggest holding companies in the world, and they're the reason she has access to this research station in the first place. They're looking to inflict some major development on the area and want to find out if, as the CFO put it, *there's anything worth selling the rights to out there.*

Kinsey was violently disinterested in the job until that same CFO told her that she could stay out here for an unprecedented four years with no oversight and no interruption in funding. A full presidential administration, with almost no limits on her scope of exploration. Four years in near isolation, with minimal temptation to distract her from work.

That's when she stopped asking questions and accepted the job. Now, she mostly tries to forget that her time here has an end date on it. She and her team will study the life that lies beneath the desert soil—the life that can be damaged by a single footfall, that could certainly be destroyed beyond salvaging by any kind of construction, that absolutely does not qualify as "anything worth selling the rights to." They'll write down everything that stands to be lost so TQI will know what it's killing.

She doubts anyone at the company will read her reports. Occasionally, briefly, she has been allowing herself to hope that TQI might forget anyone is out here at all. Maybe, she lets herself think, if no one is looking, she and her team might be able to stretch these four years into six, or eight, or ten.

Those hopes are hobbled by the physician TQI has hired to join her team. The hire is to appease TQI's insurance agency, to provide proof of the corporation's efforts to prevent fatalities in the field. There will be someone monitoring her, after all.

She'll have to make do with four years.

"Did you bring any of it with you?"

"Any what?" the new hire asks, wandering down one of the three hallways that split off from the airlock. They rap a knuckle against the wall, listening to the echo of the dead space behind it.

"Cîroc."

Their scratchy laughter echoes from halfway down the leftmost hallway, the one that leads to the lab. Kinsey follows the sound reluctantly and finds them poking their head into the exam room that will be their domain while they're at the station.

The exam room is as makeshift as everything else at the station. The drawers and cabinets are freestanding, and the exam table is a sheet of stainless steel on locking casters. It looks more like a restaurant kitchen counter than real medical equipment.

"Well? Is it everything you dreamed of?"

"I mean. It isn't set up for anything more intense than a few stitches," they reply, wandering inside. Their frame nearly fills the room. "This equipment can't save a life, which is what I'm supposed to be here for."

"We've got emergency equipment." Kinsey points to the AED that hangs on one wall.

The new doctor radiates a kind of calm confidence that leaves Kinsey feeling more stable than she did before they arrived. She frowns, determined not to like them. They turn around and lock eyes with Kinsey. "Look, Doctor Harlowe—let's you and I be honest with each other."

"Call me Kinsey."

They nod and hold out one massive, calloused hand. "Then you'll call me Mads." When they shake on it, Mads looks into Kinsey's eyes with frank candor. "Nobody here expects to be able to keep a dying person alive for the time it would take to drive to civilization and return with a medevac. I'm going to bitch at you about getting real medical supplies anyway, though, because I don't want to have a dead body on my hands. And then you'll tell TQI that I'm bitching at you, and maybe they'll send us what we need and maybe they won't. Either way, I'll be able to sleep at night knowing I did my best. Sound good?"

Kinsey looks up at them with a sinking feeling in her stomach, her hand still clasped in theirs. She can tell that, in spite of her determination not to like them, she and Mads are going to become friends. "Sounds good."

"Good." They release their grip on her and reach into one deep pocket of their coat. With a clink, they withdraw four miniature bottles of bright green Cîroc. "Now, why don't you and I get settled in?"

Over the course of the next two days, everyone gets sick except for Kinsey. The illness brings on a brief fever, a few rounds of vomiting, and a full-body rash that's gone as quickly as it comes. It could be so much worse. All told, they get off lucky.

Kinsey stays as isolated as she can while the rest of the team succumbs to the virus, but she can still hear them. Saskia and Jacques, who share the room to the right of hers, vomit for most of the first day. Domino and Nkrumah, who share the room to the left of hers, groan through the night as the rash spreads rippling pink fingers across their bodies. Mads sleeps in the room across the hall—they occupy a solo berth because they need to be able to push both twin beds together. They emerge a few times to press themself to Kinsey's door, their mouth close to the frame.

They have updates, they say. It's a fast-spreading fever, freakishly fast, almost certainly a virus. Everyone's confined to their bunks until it runs its course. The storm, they report, has taken down the landline and the Wi-Fi—not a surprise, it happens every time the dust kicks up, but the timing is bad. They release Domino from quarantine long enough to check Weatherman each morning, and the readouts seem grim—a system of sandstorms is moving toward the research station, each larger than the last. They tell her that they're feeling too ill themself to do anything beyond implementing baseline precautions and keeping the base in a state of lockdown.

Kinsey says she's fine. She says she's mostly been sleeping. Those are both lies. She hasn't been ill, but she hasn't been resting, either. She's surrounded on all sides by the thing she wants most, the thing that's always just out of reach. It's how she imagines other people feel when they see the outline of a hard nipple through a wet linen shirt: the urgency, the yearning, the delicious guilt of secret intrusion, the overwhelming weight of want.

She gets herself off over and over again to the sound of the virus trying to do its work. Her fingers ache. Everything aches. It's not enough. It doesn't matter how many times she gives herself over to the fantasy. It's not the real thing. She can never *have* the real thing.

Mads declares an end to the quarantine five days after the specimen enters the station. Everyone got sick, everyone got better, the dragon is slain, it's safe to re-emerge. Everyone, Mads announces, will need to assist with decontamination, and with shoveling sand from the storm out of the airlock—but Nkrumah puts her foot down, insisting that they should all be allowed to wash off the sticky layers of dried fever-sweat first.

The team agrees to follow their usual showering protocols, entering the dormlike double shower at the end of the residential hall in shifts. It's the same thing they do at the end of every workday, pairing up to rinse off sand and sunscreen before retiring to the canteen for a reconstituted dinner. Saskia and Mads always go first, then Jacques and Nkrumah.

Kinsey showers last, with Domino.

Domino is, above all things, irrepressible. Everyone loves them, except Jacques first thing in the morning, but then again, Jacques doesn't love anyone first thing in the morning. Domino is slow to snap, quick to joke, easy to share a lab table with. They always whistle while they shower. They're an amazing whistler so it's not annoying unless you're hungover, which is why Jacques never showers with Domino.

Kinsey listens to their trilling rendition of "Superstition" as she gingerly lathers her aching undercarriage with a palmful of Dr. Bronner's. After a moment, Domino's hand appears around the edge of the curtain. "Is the Doctor in?"

Kinsey hands the bottle over. "Careful. It's eucalyptus."

"I like the eucalyptus one best," Domino replies, conspiratorial. "Like a slap from the hand of Papa Bronner himself."

Kinsey laughs louder than she usually would. Her limbs feel loose, her thoughts soft around the edges. Exquisite soreness spirals up from the insides of her thighs to the creases of her hips. She is spent and tired and free.

Just for this moment, Kinsey is happy.

"Whew. Eucalyptus," Domino says a few minutes later when they emerge from their half of the shower, vigorously toweling their hair. "Want to go poke the specimen with me after you get dressed?"

Kinsey looks up from the puddle of leave-in conditioner in her palm. "Do I want to what?"

"The specimen. We should probably check him out."

Kinsey tilts her head to one side, combs leave-in through her hair. "Is it safe to go back into the exam room? I haven't checked with Mads about that whole decontamination thing yet. And you should stay on top of Weatherman."

"I already checked it today. No news except the same news, which is that we're stuck inside. Anyway, Mads told me it's fine. I think the specimen is kind of cute. Don't you?"

Kinsey wrinkles her nose, considering. "I don't know if I see it. I don't want to say you're wrong, but—"

When she straightens, she realizes that Domino has taken a step closer. They're standing right beside her. "Oh, Boss," they say, their voice dipping low. "Am I ever wrong?"

Kinsey feels as though her easy smile has chipped loose, detached itself from her real mouth to float an inch in front of her face. "D," she says. "What are you doing?"

She's used to fielding playful flirtation from the team. With her, they deal in the kind of goofy winking that contains not even a whisper of true invitation. Everyone knows she doesn't date, knows she's not interested in participating in their game of sexual musical chairs. They all think it's because of her professional boundaries—she's mentioned more than once that since she's the team lead, it would be unethical for her to donate her orifices to the office potluck.

Maybe some of them think there's more to it—that she's asexual, or that she's secretly monogamously married, or that she took some kind of vow of celibacy in her wayward youth. Most of the time she doesn't concern herself with the possibility of their speculation, because what matters is that everyone respects her blanket *no thanks*. Everyone knows where she stands.

Nobody ever gives her the kind of look that Domino is giving her now.

"What do you want me to be doing?" Domino asks, their voice rough. Their tongue slips forward to slide slowly across their front teeth. Kinsey's eyes are drawn by the movement, then snagged by something that doesn't look right.

Kinsey has never paid much attention to any of her colleagues' tongues, but she knows she'd remember if one of them had a snakelike fork at the tip.

Domino's tongue stills, as though caught by her gaze. After a few seconds it vanishes again, reeled back into the dark cavern of their mouth. Kinsey forces herself to meet Domino's eyes again.

They take another half step closer. There wasn't a half step's worth of space between them and Kinsey before, and now they're pressed together airtight. She can feel the quick drum of Domino's heartbeat where their chest is mashed against her arm. Just as she draws breath to speak—to ask a question that hasn't fully formed in her mind yet—Domino lets out a too-loud laugh.

"You wouldn't believe the look on your face," they crow. "Honestly, Boss, you need to loosen up. You've got goose bumps."

They grab her shoulders, give her a little shake. The sudden movement loosens the twist in her towel, and she clutches at the cloth to keep it from slipping off her breasts. She's been naked in front of Domino so many times. Hell, they were the one to pull a tick off her nipple when she couldn't stomach doing it herself. It shouldn't matter.

But something is different now. Their hands are still on her shoulders and their palms are pressed close to her skin and their eyes keep dropping to her lips and they're laughing, but the laugh isn't quite right.

More than any of that, Kinsey is troubled by how much she wants to see that forked tongue again. But she knows that's impossible, because the forked tongue wasn't real. She imagined it. She turns away from them, runs a shaky hand through her damp hair, tells herself to get her shit together. "You're right. I need to loosen up. Let's go poke a dead thing, huh?"

"Sounds like a date," Domino says. They head for the door and whistle their way down the hall toward the room they share with Nkrumah.

Kinsey doesn't follow until she hears their door close.

The specimen is exactly where Kinsey saw it last. The edges of the exam room door are sealed with multiple layers of duct tape, and there's a torn half sheet of printer paper taped to the window that says *don't virus open inside* in Mads's handwriting.

"Do you think it's safe to go in there?" Kinsey says, as if the sign isn't clear on that question.

"Definitely," Domino replies. They shoot her a lopsided grin, tug at the collar of their floral button-down shirt. "It's just a virus, Boss. It can't hurt you."

Kinsey frowns. She knows that the logic of what Domino just said doesn't follow—of course a virus can hurt her, it can hurt anyone. But it feels right, what they've said. It's always felt right. Some part of her, deep down in a place that can't access reason, believes that viruses really *can't* hurt her. Or maybe it's more accurate to say that she believes viruses *won't* hurt her—that the strength of her desire, the force of her love, would be enough to make them treat her differently from everybody else.

That belief is part of what made her seek out remote research postings in the first place. She needed some distance from the constant waves of viral illnesses that kept washing over all of humanity. It was too hard to make herself get the vaccines and wear the masks and bathe her hands in sanitizer—to enforce that distance between herself and the thing that made her entire body pulse with desire. She couldn't stand the sound of her neighbor coughing on the other side of her thin apartment walls. The knowledge that if she just put her tongue into that neighbor's mouth for a few seconds, she could have their virus inside her body.

She couldn't keep waging the war between the part of her mind that knew she could die from something like that—and the part of her heart that was absolutely certain she wouldn't.

She's never heard anyone else put voice to that feeling. *It's just a virus. It can't hurt you.* She waits for Domino to laugh, to give her some sign that they're joking, but they don't.

Kinsey gestures to the duct-tape-sealed door. "After you," she says. Once they're inside, she pauses. "Huh. Did Mads already do their decontamination thing in this wing?"

"Hm? Oh, probably. Why?"

"It should fucking reek in here. Wonder what gives," she says as she pulls a fistful of blue nitrile gloves from the wall-mounted dispenser, a hard-won concession from TQI after the first month of Mads's campaign for basic personal protective equipment.

"Why would it reek?"

She doesn't bother trying to hide her what's-wrong-with-you reaction to Domino's question. "There's been a corpse in here for days, is why. And you're being weirdly casual about this whole mystery virus. Why aren't you more worried?"

She double-layers her gloves, reaches inside the disposable gown box where she only finds a startled daddy longlegs. Debates whether it's necessary to bother with a mask. Decides, with a flirtatious flush of rebellious impulsivity, against. What does it matter if she leaves her mouth nude, once she's already kissed the contaminated air?

"Don't call it that."

"What?" Kinsey turns to find Domino looking at her with startling vulnerability.

"Don't call it a corpse. It was alive when we brought it inside. It might still be alive now."

Kinsey turns to regard the specimen. It lies limp on the tarp, precisely where she left it. Its segmented body has a wasp-narrow waist, the barrel chest and wide pelvis on either side of that waist forming a stark hourglass. It's on its side, all six of its long multi-jointed legs tangled together, its coyote-head lolling at an ecstatic angle.

It looks like a dead saint, Kinsey thinks. Operative word: *dead*. It's not moving, not breathing, not turning to fix her with a hypnotizing eyeless gaze.

But if Domino doesn't want her using the C word, so be it. "What would you prefer me to call the specimen? A body?"

"You could call it by a name, if you wanted. You could call it anything," Domino says. "It really is safe to be in here, Kinsey. You can feel that, can't you? It wouldn't hurt you."

They seem serious enough that Kinsey doesn't know how to react. She doesn't want to go along with the joke, but now she's not sure that it actually *is* a joke, and she doesn't know how to ask. "Did Weatherman indicate a break in the storm anytime soon? Maybe we can just take this thing back outside." She doesn't want to take it back outside.

"Nah," Domino replies lightly. "We should keep it in here. And we should all stay inside just in case, too. Do you need me to take notes?"

Kinsey gives herself a shake, tells herself not to worry. "Yeah, that'd be great. Do you want a laptop or a notebook or . . . anything?"

Domino shakes their head. "I'll remember. I remember everything you do, Boss."

"What's that supposed to mean?"

"I pay close attention. I love watching you work," they add, their gaze flicking down over her body. "What are you going to do to the specimen?"

Kinsey has spent her entire adult life ignoring her instincts. She knows better than to listen to her body when it tells her what it wants, what it needs, what it yearns for. But it's screaming at her now, too loud to ignore. Something is happening that she doesn't like. Something in the way Domino is looking at her, something in the way they're talking to her.

When she asks herself if she needs to do something about it, she finds no clear answers. There's discomfort, yes, and confusion—but also something she's never felt toward another human before. A muted, distant sense of desire.

She turns away from Domino so fast that she stumbles, catching herself on the edge of the exam table. The tarp crinkles under her palm. "I'm going to examine it," she snaps. "That's what we're here to do."

"Do you like it?" Domino asks. Their voice comes from just behind her left ear, their breath warm on her neck. Kinsey glances sideways to find their face just inches from hers. "Do you like how it looks, I mean?"

"Yes," Kinsey answers without thinking, turning back to the specimen. "It's fascinating." She reaches one gloved hand toward it, strokes the bristly fur on its flank. Sand rains down out of its coat, falling onto the tarp with a soft patter that sounds just like the earliest wind of the sandstorm against Kinsey's bedroom wall.

"What do you like about it?"

Kinsey still doesn't trust this—doesn't trust Domino's warmth against her back or the frank seduction in their voice—but she doesn't tell them to stop, either. She looks over the specimen, studies the shape of it. "It's unique," she says. "It's ours."

"Ours," Domino repeats. She feels light pressure at her waist and looks down to see their hands resting on her hips.

"D," she says, her hand still resting on the specimen. "Don't."

"Don't what?" they breathe, so close she can taste their teeth.

"Don't. I mean it," she says, even though for the first time in her life, she's not entirely sure that she *does* mean it. It must be the specimen, she tells herself, the anxiety of proximity to the thing, combined with the residual crotchache that comes with three days of nonstop masturbation. She tells herself that she's confused. Of course she doesn't want Domino.

They tug on one of her hips, spinning her slowly around

to face them. They look down at her with puzzled, wounded eyes. "You don't, though. You don't mean it."

"I can and I do. Let go of me," she says. She tries to put force behind the words, tries to will away the bizarre frisson of desire that keeps stirring in her.

But Domino doesn't let go. "I know you like me," they insist. "Why are you acting like you don't?"

"I don't like you, not . . . not like this." She raises her hands to their chest, intending to push them away—but stops. Something under their shirt is moving. "What—"

"What don't you like? I can fix it," they insist.

The movement under her hands doesn't stop. It's a restless pulsating push, like something fighting to get out from beneath the cloth. "D," she breathes. She means it with concern but it comes out wrong, like the whisper of a lover, and she sees them hear it wrong, feels them press closer to her in response.

"I can fix it," they say again. "You like my mouth, right? I saw you looking at it earlier. You like this." They flick their tongue out, run it across their bottom lip, and Kinsey realizes that she wasn't confused or hallucinating when she noticed it earlier. It's forked and flat, quick and flexible, *reptile*.

"Your tongue," she says, and again it comes out all wrong. She can see it on Domino's face—they don't hear horror. They hear lust.

They lick their lips again, slower this time. "This," they say. "You like this. That's good. I can work with that."

The pulsing movement inside their shirt turns into a ripple of flesh. She jerks away from them, slamming the small of her back into the metal edge of the exam table. It slides away with a screech of stainless steel on linoleum.

She hears a crinkle, a slide of plastic over metal, a *whump* as the specimen falls to the floor.

But she doesn't turn to look. She can't take her eyes off Domino. Their shirt is visibly moving now, something writhing beneath the fabric. Something spreading.

"Just give me a few minutes and I'll fix it," they say insistently. Their tongue flicks out of their mouth again, tasting the air as they look down at their own chest. They start undoing their shirt buttons with clumsy, trembling fingers. "You're going to love this. I promise."

Kinsey wants to run, but her legs won't move. She drags herself along the edge of the exam table, willing herself to bolt for the door. *You said no, and Domino isn't listening,* she thinks. *Domino isn't listening and they are taking their shirt off. They are taking their shirt off and you need to* run.

But Domino isn't pursuing her. Domino isn't even touching her. Domino is unbuttoning their shirt and their eyes are wide with what looks for all the world like genuine hope, and something is moving under that shirt, and some part of Kinsey, some part of her that is stronger than her thinking mind, wants to stay and see it.

Three buttons in, Domino lets out a growl of impatience, then rips their way through the rest. One button flies off and hits Kinsey in the chest, but she doesn't care. She doesn't even feel it.

"There," they breathe, looking up at her with an open, earnest grin. "That. You like that, right?"

Kinsey has no words, because she knows now what was shifting beneath her hand.

Domino's chest has erupted into a rash of mouths. Pillowy lips and blunt white teeth. Each one opens invitingly, revealing a warm wet darkness within. As she watches, the mouth closest to Domino's collarbone stretches wide. A raw wad of new pink flesh pinches itself up out of that darkness, stretching and writhing to form a tongue just like the one in the mouth on their face.

"Well?" They look up at her with unadulterated hope. "Do you like that?"

Kinsey wishes she didn't.

The video on Kinsey's laptop judders as the hotel Wi-Fi throttles her signal. She sits in her room, drumming her fingers on the smearless glass of the desk, waiting for the candidate's image to clear. "Can you see me?"

"I—see—can—?" Their voice comes through in robotic bursts.

Kinsey sighs and hangs up the call. She's unwilling to wait. TQI is bringing her to their Albuquerque headquarters for some kind of paperwork bonanza, and she only has half an hour before the car they're sending will ping her phone to tell her it's pulling up. If she's going to arrive with her first hire under her belt, she needs to be able to talk to the candidate now.

Her cell phone hotspot does the job better than the

hotel internet was ever going to. She calls them back, and this time, they're at least recognizable as a human being.

The conversation picks up quickly. The candidate jokes easily, apologizes after swearing and then immediately swears again, drops hints about hating TQI but loving the sound of the work. Kinsey is charmed. She asks questions about their research into dune ecology and wind patterns, and then gets into some specifics about their experience with Weatherman. Everyone at the station will be doing a bit of everything, but this person will take point on storm tracking; it will be their job to decipher the steady stream of weather data that will come into the base via satellite. They tell her about their love for the red glow of the screen when the incoming data indicates severe conditions.

When Kinsey asks the candidate if they have questions for her, they ask what she's most excited to research out there in the desert.

"Me?"

Domino nods. "You're the team lead. I want to know what you're there to look for. Or are you just excited to make some sand angels and get a tan?"

She feels clumsy, trying to explain. She's tired from the flight. But she tries anyway. "The thing about the desert is, it's alive."

On the screen, Domino nods politely. "Right, the ecological landscape is rich with—"

Kinsey waves a hand to cut them off. "Not like that. It's—it's alive. The desert itself. The whole thing. There's the sand, right?" She holds a hand out flat, palm down. Then she points to the space beneath her hand. "But just down here, like five inches below the sand that you can see with your eyes—it's alive. The entire desert. There's this layer called the cryptobiotic crust. It's all one huge living interconnected thing, made of algae and moss and bacteria and lichens—"

"Lichens?" There's a spark in Domino's eye already, just as Kinsey knew there'd be. Everyone loves lichens.

"Oh, yeah. Like you wouldn't believe," she says, the warm thrill of her work building in her. She loves this. She never spends enough time around people to get to talk about it. "And it's active. It soaks up water and it forms these filament networks that keep all the sand from blowing away, and it *breathes,* and it's—"

Domino leans in close to their webcam, their eyes gleaming. "I'm in."

"What?"

"I'm in. I'll take the job."

Kinsey half laughs, startled, and doubly startled to find herself delighted. "I didn't offer you the job y—"

"When do I start?"

Kinsey eyes Mads. "You can read Weatherman, right? You'll know when it's safe for us to go outside?" She wants to be able to tell her team to leave. She wants to be able to tell them to run.

"Kind of," they reply warily. "Domino has tried to teach me a few times. It mostly just looks like static to me, though. I'll look at it again when we're done with... whatever this is." They're next to Kinsey, staring through the wire-reinforced window. "I don't understand why you two were in the exam room in the first place, and I *really* don't understand why Domino has to stay in there."

"It's not like that door locks," Kinsey says. "They can come out whenever they want."

Mads glances at the layers of fresh duct tape that crisscross the exam room door. Kinsey isn't sure how much she used. Most of the roll is gone, but maybe there wasn't that much left to begin with. She couldn't be sure, that's what she kept repeating to herself over and over as she tried to make a seal over the door, to cocoon Domino inside with the specimen. She needed to make sure.

They didn't try to fight her, didn't try to escape. They just stood there, asking her over and over to tell them what they'd done wrong.

"The thing is," Mads says in a voice one might use to try to pacify a loose baboon, "I don't see the problem you're saying you saw."

"I'm not crazy," Kinsey snaps.

"I didn't say you were crazy."

"That's what people say when they think you're crazy," Nkrumah chimes in. She's standing far from the exam room window, her back pressed to the opposite wall.

"I'm with Mads," Jacques says. He's halfway between Nkrumah and the window. His hands are stuffed into his pockets. Every time he speaks, the smell of wintergreen mouthwash drifts across the little vestibule. "She's crazy."

"I didn't say she's crazy," Mads says, sharper this time. "I just said that I don't see the . . . the lips."

"Mouths." Kinsey doesn't look away from Domino. They're staring out through the window with wet, beseeching eyes, radiating innocence. *They're tricking everyone*, Kinsey thinks. It sends waves of fury washing through her. "They were covered in mouths, Mads. You tell me what medical condition makes that happen, and *then* I'll calm down."

"Psychosis," Saskia says mildly. "Could cause this, I mean."

"Putting that social work minor to good use," Jacques mutters. He always gets a little mean when he's stressed.

Saskia smiles as if she doesn't hear the sarcasm in his

tone. "Yes, I am. It's okay, Kinsey. Lots of people experience hallucinations. You've been isolated here with us for so long, and that fever was no joke—nobody would fault you if—"

"I didn't hallucinate it," Kinsey interrupts. She doesn't add that she never got the fever. They don't need to know that part. "I didn't."

Saskia shrugs. "How would you know if you were hallucinating? You'd reality-test by asking people you trust if what you saw was real, right?" The question sounds genuine. Sincere. That's how she is—brisk, but earnestly nonjudgmental. Kinsey knows that Saskia genuinely wouldn't think less of her if this thing with Domino really was all in her head.

And she's got a point. If Kinsey's not sure what she's seeing, she asks her team. That's always been the case. When she thinks someone might be pissed or depressed, she asks Mads to look at it. When she needs to send a dubious email to corporate headquarters, she turns to Nkrumah. When she isn't sure if it's safe outside, she gets Domino's take.

But this is different. This time, she doesn't need anyone's confirmation, because she doesn't doubt what she saw. Not in the slightest.

"Tell you what," Nkrumah offers. "Let's take another look. We'll all look, hard as we can, with absolutely no prior assumptions about what we might see. And if there are no lips—"

"Mouths," Kinsey insists.

"Right. Mouths. If there are no mouths, we'll let Domino out, and we'll talk things over as a team. Okay?"

Kinsey chews the inside of her lip for a moment before the feel of her lip between her teeth reminds her too much of what she saw under Domino's shirt. She looks at her team—Mads, giant and reasonable; Jacques, blurry-eyed but loyal; Saskia, anxious but faithful; Nkrumah, self-assured and honest to a fault.

They're all she has. The world is a hundred miles away, across an expanse of sand that would kill her without noticing she'd ever been alive. If she can't lean on her team, she's already done for.

She nods once. "Okay."

They gather close to her, crowding in around the window. Domino hasn't moved. Their expression hasn't changed. That, Kinsey thinks, should be proof enough. Domino is constantly in motion. They always have something to say. But now they're silent as they watch and wait for everyone else to decide whether or not they're a monster.

Mads presses closer to her to make room for Saskia. On Kinsey's other side, Jacques and Nkrumah cram themselves together to look into the exam room window. Mads taps on the glass, and even though Domino was already looking in that direction, their expression sharpens.

"Hey D," Mads calls. "I know this sucks, but it'll be over soon, okay? Can you just, uh. Sorry about this," they add, apparently realizing what they have to ask and how it's going to sound. "But can you take your shirt off for us? Or just stop holding the front shut, maybe?"

Kinsey shakes her head. "Off," she insists. She doesn't want them to be able to hide anything.

Domino walks toward the window. They come close, unreasonably close, so close that their breath fogs the glass.

"Kinsey," they say softly. "This is nuts. Just let me out, and we can talk this over. I know I probably came on too strong—"

"Wait, you really made a move on Kinsey?" Jacques interrupts, sounding more than a little betrayed.

"That's a wild choice," Nkrumah says. "Like . . . it's Kinsey. You don't—"

Mads cuts her off. "The shirt, D," they say, firmer this time. "Please."

Domino hesitates. Their grip on the fabric is tight. "I don't want to."

"We shouldn't make them if they don't want to," Saskia says.

Kinsey slams her palm against the glass. Everyone jumps at the noise. Everyone except Domino. "I don't care what they want," she hisses. "I didn't want to be backed into that exam table. You think the specimen fell down all by itself? I knocked it over while I was trying to get away from them."

"You didn't want to get away from me," Domino murmurs.

Nkrumah looks across Jacques at the rest of the team. "What did they say?"

"She can't hear me," Domino says again, even softer this time. Their eyes are locked onto Kinsey's, their lips barely moving. As she watches, their pupils slowly shrink to pinpoints. "But you can, can't you? You know why," they add. "We have a bond. Me and you, Kinsey."

Kinsey slams her palm against the window again. "Take the fucking shirt off," she yells. Spittle flies from her mouth, flecking the glass in front of her.

Domino's lips twitch upward at the corners, the faintest ghost of a smile. "Sure. No problem. I just wanted it to be you who was asking."

They twitch the fabric apart, letting it fall open to reveal a scant sliver of deep bronze flesh. Kinsey's heart stutters at the sight. She doesn't understand her own reaction—can't understand it—hates it. She doesn't want Domino. She isn't *attracted* to Domino. So why does she feel the urge to run her tongue across that sliver of flesh?

They tug the shirt off one shoulder, coy. They run their finger across the length of one collarbone, nudging the collar of their shirt until it falls off their shoulder. The sleeves of their shirt fall to the crooks of their elbows and they hug it around themself, turn their back and wiggle their shoulders like a burlesque dancer.

Saskia lets out a breathy laugh. Kinsey glances over and sees that Mads is wearing an indulgent smile. All of them think that Domino is taking this ridiculous interrogation with good humor, she realizes. They think their colleague is being a good sport in the face of the boss's obvious derangement.

She digs her fingernails into the meat of her palms. They'll see. They have to see.

Finally, after a long striptease, Domino lets their shirt drift to the floor. They stand in front of the exam room window, half-naked, their arms held out, their palms up. They haven't lost that easy smile, that open gaze. Everything about them radiates innocence.

Kinsey feels Mads freeze beside her. She glances up and sees that their wry smile has vanished, replaced by a perfectly blank expression. She looks back at Domino, then lifts a finger and gives it a grim twirl. "Arms up," she says, "and spin."

Domino lets their head drop to one side, the perfect picture of bemused exasperation. They turn once, slowly, their hands above their head. "See anything you like?"

Kinsey glances around at her team again. Saskia's face

has drained of what little color it had. Nkrumah's lips have vanished, pressed tight into her mouth. Jacques looks like he needs to get to the nearest trash can.

"Thanks, Dom," Mads says at last, completely unreadable. "You can put your shirt back on."

"And then I can come out?" Domino asks plaintively.

"We need to talk to Kinsey first," Mads replies. "Get her calmed down, maybe sedated. Then, yes, we'll take the tape off the door and you can come out."

Kinsey's gut twists as she looks up at Mads, searching for an explanation in their face. "But—"

"Come on," Mads says firmly, grabbing Kinsey by the elbow and tugging her toward the hallway. "Let's get you settled. Team, will you help me with her?"

"Sure thing." Nkrumah takes Kinsey's other elbow.

Jacques and Saskia come with them, Jacques ahead and Saskia behind. Kinsey can hear Saskia murmuring a prayer under her breath. She lets herself be guided away from the exam room, too stunned to fight her team. "What the fuck," she hisses. "Are you guys for real right now? You didn't see that?"

"Of course we saw it," Mads sighs.

Jacques, walking a step ahead, drops his head into his hands. "I don't know what I saw," he mumbles. "I don't—I don't think I saw anything."

Nkrumah reaches out an arm and rubs his back briskly, like she's trying to restore circulation to his entire spine. "C'mon," she says. "You did so."

"Yeah, I did," he agrees. "I just wish I didn't. I—you know how I feel about them, and I don't want..." He doesn't find an end to his sentence.

Saskia keeps praying.

Kinsey could weep with relief. That she isn't alone—that

her team is with her—that Domino didn't manage to fool anyone. "So you saw it too. All of you. It's not just me." She knows she's saying the same thing over and over again, but she can't seem to stop. Nobody answers her until after they've made their way down the hall and into the canteen, in the center spoke of the wedge. The second they walk into the canteen, Mads and Nkrumah release Kinsey's elbows. She wheels around on them. "Say it," she says desperately. "Say you saw it."

"They weren't mouths," Nkrumah points out.

Jacques groans. "Worse than mouths, I think. Eyes are worse than mouths."

Mads shakes their head. "Not eyes," they say. They don't sound shaken at all—but then again, they never do. "Just eyelids."

That's what had been under Domino's shirt. Not on their chest—that was normal again, a smooth expanse of skin slashed by dark scars below each nipple, a scattering of freckles and hair running down the centerline of their sternum. There was no sign that there had ever been a cluster of open, inviting mouths there. For a moment, Kinsey had worried that Saskia had been right—that it had all been a hallucination.

But then Domino had let their shirt drop, and Kinsey had felt the terrible weight of certainty land in her stomach. There was their belly—a sweet curve of soft skin, usually broken only by their navel and the glint of the jeweled piercing they wore in it.

But now the belly ring was gone, replaced by a perfectly formed, long-lashed eyelid.

There were two more navels flanking the original. All three were shuttered by identical eyelids. As Kinsey had watched, they'd winked slowly, one by one. When Domino had raised their arms, they'd revealed smaller ones, follicular and close-clustered. Each underarm was a lotus pod of empty eyelashed sockets.

Kinsey had stared into those eyes, and she had felt it. She didn't know how, but she was certain.

They'd been staring right back at her.

The end of the team's first full week at the research station coincides with their first sandstorm. Weatherman fills the lab with warm red light, which Domino translates into news of incoming danger. The wind outside screams against the walls of the station. The lab wing and the residential wing both feel exposed, thanks to their exterior walls. Over the course of the day, the entire team has drifted into the canteen, where the outside world feels a little more removed.

Jacques is the last to enter. He arrived at the station the same time as Saskia, the two of them joining the rest of the team the day before the storm. He shivers as he walks into the canteen. It's eternally chilly in here, since there aren't any exterior walls letting in heat. The air conditioner is always working overtime to keep the residential wing and the lab wing cool, but the canteen has an entire storage room between it and the elements outside, so it gets refrigerated by the overactive cooling system.

"Hope you're nearly done with that blanket," he says, nodding to Saskia as he passes through the canteen. She's sitting on one of the beat-up secondhand sofas and armchairs that form a rash around the scarred coffee table. The first few inches of a knitted blanket hang between her fingers.

"Oh, sure. Just a few more minutes," she murmurs. Domino is the only one who catches the joke. The laugh they let out is loud and sudden enough that it startles Mads into dropping their pristine copy of *Tropic of Cancer*.

Nothing in the canteen is fully attached to the walls, not even the sink. Bulk-bought shelf-stable food is stacked on wire shelves lining the walls. Jacques bypasses them and opens the storage closet at the back of the canteen. "What's in here?"

The sound of the wind outside invades the room. "Sandstorm. Don't let it out," Nkrumah calls. She's sitting next to the coffee table, laying out cards for a complicated version of solitaire that she refuses to explain to the others.

Jacques disappears into the closet. He emerges again a moment later with a handle of dark rum in one hand and a bag of limes in the other. "Jackpot."

"Jaques-pot," Domino corrects. "Where you headed with all those limes?"

Jacques kicks the storage closet door shut behind him, dropping the room back into relative peace. "We're all stuck in here tonight. Tomorrow morning too, probably. So I figure we should have a good time while we're at it. Tomorrow, I think we should see about knocking out some of the walls between things. So much wasted space. But not tonight. What do you say, Boss? Cocktails?"

Kinsey stands up, walks to the stack of heavy-duty plastic bins that hold the team's dishware. She pops the lid off the bin that holds the mugs, pulls one out, uses the tail of her shirt to wipe dust out of it.

"That seems like a yes?" he says, using his thumb to break the seal on top of the handle of rum.

Kinsey holds her mug out to him. "Let's fucking party."

He takes it with an approving nod and starts to pour as the others rummage for their own mugs. Once everyone has a full pour, a healthy squeeze of lime, and a splash of the watery ginger ale Mads pulls out of the storage closet, Jacques raises his mug for a toast. "To sandstorms."

The rest of them follow suit. "To sandstorms!"

Mads takes charge. Kinsey knows she should be thankful for that—she's in no state to decide what the team should do next, can't be even the slightest bit objective about Domino. But she's not thankful. She's embarrassed. It's degrading. She's supposed to lead this team, she's supposed to know what she's doing. She's the one who decides their next steps.

But she can't right now, can she? Her legs are shaking and she can't feel her fingers all the way and every time she looks at the freestanding kitchenette in the corner of the canteen, some part of her insists that she should stick her hand down the drain and turn on the garbage disposal. She knows that pureeing her hand wouldn't fix anything, but it would create a new problem, and at least if she's dealing with a new problem she isn't dealing with *this* problem.

"We need to find out what's happening to Dom," Mads says, tugging one of Saskia's many blankets across their shoulders. "We need to know what's causing the . . . the symptoms."

"The eyes," Jacques corrects. He stands up abruptly and walks over to the kitchenette. Kinsey thinks for a moment that he might be about to do the garbage disposal thing himself—maybe it's not such a bad idea after all?—but then he opens a cabinet and removes a half-empty handle of white rum. He sloshes some of it into a mug without pretending to consider how much he's pouring. "The eyes," he says again, ripping open a packet of powdered apple cider mix and dumping it into the mug. He stirs with his finger, then takes a long drink.

"That can't taste good," Kinsey whispers.

Saskia frowns. "I don't think it even dissolved all the way."

Nkrumah leans forward and slaps her palm down onto the coffee table. "That's why we have to figure out what's wrong with Domino."

Everyone looks at her with equal confusion. "What," Saskia says, "because Jacques is drinking sludge?"

"Because maybe it's not dissolved all the way," Nkrumah says. Her eyes are alight with hope. "Maybe whatever's in them, we can get it out again."

"You're not getting the powder out of this rum," Jacques says, licking his teeth. "It's not dissolved all the way, but it's not the same as it was, you know? They're part of the same fucked-up thing now. We have to accept it."

The ceiling overhead rattles and all of them look up, startled.

"Can't be another sandstorm already, can it?" Kinsey mutters.

"What's Weatherman say?" Saskia asks.

They all look at each other, blank-faced. Jacques sighs and walks to the door with his mug of sludge. "I'll just take a look outside."

"Be careful," Mads says, running their broad, blunt-fingered hands across their face. "Nkrumah's right," they say. "We gotta see if we can help Dom. They have to be hurting right now. Kinsey, I know you're upset," they add, "but you and I both know that none of this is how Domino would act if they were in their right mind."

"I know." She's not sure if that's true or not, but she knows it's the right sound to make, so she makes it.

They all sit in silence until Jacques returns to the room, his now-empty mug hanging at his side in one slack hand. His face is grim. "It's another one. And it looks big."

"How big?" Nkrumah asks.

Before Jacques can answer, the ceiling rattles again, harder this time. It sounds like a giant is banging on the roof with one furious fist, trying to get inside.

"No fieldwork for the next day or so, that's for sure," he answers. "It's still on the horizon but the wind's already here, so I figure it's a big one. Can't imagine it'll be gentle."

"So we're stuck inside. Wi-Fi and phone lines are still down, and nobody's going to come fix anything with another storm rolling through. The only person who can read Weatherman reliably is covered in eyelids, so we can't risk fieldwork between storms, either. That makes this an easy decision—we'll focus on Domino, since we can't do shit else anyhow. We'll go back to the exam room and get some samples from them," Mads says. They sound so reasonable. It makes Kinsey want to hit them. "You all do what you do best. You examine, you study, you identify, you catalog. And then I get to do what I do best. I treat them."

"And then they're back to normal," Kinsey says, trying not to sound regretful.

Saskia nods. "And we all forget this ever happened."

When the team returns to their vantage point outside the exam room window, Domino is sitting cross-legged in the center of the room. They're wearing their button-down again. It hangs open in the front, loose. Kinsey scans what she can see of their skin and spots no eyes, no mouths, nothing out of the ordinary. Panic flutters briefly beneath her collarbones—what if her team rescinds their belief in her, what if they decide it was all just a moment of shared delusion?—but then she looks up at Domino's face, and her worry vanishes.

There's no denying that something's wrong with them. Their expression no longer has the open, earnest guilelessness it had before, when they were insisting that Kinsey was imagining things. Now, their typically animated face is utterly still, their eyes flat as dropped pennies.

Jacques shakes his head slowly at the sight of them. "Something's not right," he mutters. "That ain't them."

"So," Domino says to the gathered team. "That was embarrassing."

Mads addresses them first. "No need to be embarrassed, D. You're sick, that's all. Can I come into the room?"

"Nah." Their mouth snaps into a too-wide grin. Kinsey counts three canines on each side. "But Kinsey can."

Nkrumah grabs Kinsey's arm down low, where Domino won't be able to see. "Don't," she whispers through clenched teeth. Then, louder: "I'll go."

"No," Domino and Mads say in unison.

Nkrumah leans across Kinsey to glare at Mads. "What the fuck," she hisses.

"You can't go in and neither can Kinsey," Mads replies levelly. "Neither of you knows how to take a tissue sample—"

"We do so," Kinsey says, momentarily more indignant than she is afraid.

"—*from a living person*," Mads finishes. "Domino's not a specimen you found out in the field. They're alive. They can still feel pain."

Saskia scoffs. "If they could still feel pain, we would have heard them screaming when they grew eyes on their stomach."

Mads frowns. "We can't know what that felt like. Best practice in a moment like this one is to assume—you know what? I don't have to explain this to you. I'm the doctor here."

Inside the exam room, Domino pushes themself to their feet. They stretch, yawn, scratch the back of their neck. Sand falls from their shoulders as they move. Kinsey can't tell where it came from. They move toward the exam table, leaving a trail of grit behind them. They look down at the specimen, which is still sprawled out on top of the tarp on the floor.

"Not my best work," they mutter. Then they stoop and lift the specimen—the specimen it took three people to lift just a few days before. In their arms now, it looks like it weighs nothing at all. They heft it easily over one shoulder, then drop it onto the exam table.

A gust of wind shakes the wall of the corridor behind the team. Sand whips against the building, making a sound like a thousand fingernails tapping impatiently. Everyone turns to look except Kinsey, who can't take her eyes off

Domino. They glance up, see her staring. Their mouth twitches like they're holding back a smile.

"I'll go," Kinsey hears herself say.

Domino's mouth barely moves, but she can hear them anyway. "Attagirl."

She adjusts the wireless headphone in her ear, even though it doesn't need adjusting. The feel of the smooth plastic under the pad of her finger reminds her that she's not alone. She pulls a handful of gloves off the wall, double-layers just like always. Tightens the nose bridge on her facemask.

"I wish you wouldn't do that," Domino murmurs. "You don't need gloves. Not with me."

Kinsey clears her throat, turns her back on them, double-checks that the walkie-talkie clipped to her belt is on. "It's procedure."

"Please. You don't know what procedure is. You've never done anything like this before, have you, Kinsey?"

There's a beep in one headphone. She presses her finger to it again, harder this time. A soft click, and then Mads is in her ear.

"You okay?"

When she doesn't reply, they clear their throat. She glances over to see Mads watching her through the window, their face tight with concern, the walkie-talkie in their hand just out of sight below the windowsill. "Right. Let's take some samples."

She's already got most of what she needs. But Domino is right: she's never used these tools on a living creature before. It was strange, removing them from her field kit to bring into this room. It's stranger still to think that she'll be using them on a member of her own team.

"Kinsey, will you look at me?" Domino's voice is terribly gentle. "It sounds like there's another storm coming. Is that right?"

"Seems like it."

"Hard to get details when your Weatherman interpreter's locked in the nurse's office. Best to stay inside." Domino's mouth twitches, like they're about to kiss the air.

Kinsey swallows around the painful lump that's forming in her throat. That's the second time Domino has suggested that everyone should stay inside. "Give me a second."

Mads comes to life in her ear. "For what?"

Kinsey gives her head a minute shake. "How should I start?"

After a moment's silence, Mads answers. "Ask Domino to take the shirt off again."

"Shirt off," she says, turning her back on them. She hears the sound of Domino's shirt shushing across their skin, then hitting the floor. After a second, she hears a zipper too. "You can keep the pants on," she says.

"Why? Don't you need to inspect all of me?" There's a playful tilt in Domino's voice. "Don't be scared to look, Kinsey. I promise not to make eyes at you again."

Kinsey isn't an angry person as a rule. She tries not to get angry now. "No jokes," she says. "Please. I need to concentrate." Then, before she can hesitate a second longer, she picks up a sterile large-gauge needle and syringe. She turns and forces herself to look Domino square in the face, holding the needle aloft like the weapon it might need to be.

They look exactly the way they're supposed to look. They look like her colleague, like the person she's spent years laughing with and digging next to and falling asleep on and teasing and snapping at and showering with. Every part of them looks perfectly normal.

But the way she's *seeing* them isn't normal. Not for her. Her eyes trail across their skin and she can feel a lift in her belly, the rise of goosebumps across her arms, the prickle of rising hairs on the back of her neck. She runs a tongue across her lower lip before she knows she's even doing it.

Kinsey grips the needle tighter. She's sure of it now: she wants Domino. She wants to grab them and sink her teeth into them. She wants them to pin her wrists above her head and have their way with her. She wants to know the taste of their sweat and their blood and she wants to scream their name so loud it makes coyotes twenty miles from here start to yip in response, she wants them to—

"No," she says aloud.

"No?" Mads and Domino say, one in her ear and one in the room.

She clears her throat. "No, I don't need to examine all of you," she says. Against her will, her eyes drop to the tight boxer-briefs Domino wears. "Just the areas where the symptoms occurred."

Domino winces. "I'm sorry about that," they whisper. "Really. I'm mortified. It's just—I'm not used to being like this yet, and it's confusing, trying to figure out where everything belongs."

"You're not making any sense," Kinsey says.

"Aphasia," Mads says in her ear. "Could be a mini-stroke, could be some kind of brain damage from that fever. Encephalitis, maybe. Keep your mask on just in case."

Kinsey knows what aphasia is. She still remembers when her father lost the power of coherent speech after his last stroke. It didn't sound anything like this. "Gotta be something like that," she says anyway.

At Mads's instruction, Kinsey sets the pre-wrapped, single-use syringe down on a tray alongside gauze, medical tape, a pile of pre-packed alcohol wipes. She asks Domino to lie flat on the exam table. She positions them carefully, handling their limbs as gently as she knows how, avoiding their gaze for as long as she can.

After a few minutes of Kinsey's bustling, Domino speaks. "Hey. Can you look at me? In the eyes? They're up here this time," Domino says, a joke hidden somewhere in the recesses of their voice. "No? Kinsey. Come on."

She shakes her head, picks up the syringe, drops it again when the wind makes the building shiver. "Fuck. I'm doing this all backward." She tears open a foil packet with a large alcohol swab inside. "I need to focus, okay? You have to let me pay attention to what I'm doing, or I'll hurt you."

"I promise you can't hurt me," Domino murmurs. Kinsey flinches as they reach up to her. They press their index finger to the underside of her chin and tug gently, pulling her chin toward them until she can't help but meet their gaze. "There," they say. "That's better."

"What are you?" Kinsey whispers. Her voice doesn't tremble, but it feels like a voice-trembling question all the same.

"I'm yours," Domino replies.

Kinsey's lips part. She doesn't mean them to, but they do. She presses them back together hard, jerks her head away from Domino's hand. "I need to take this sample," she says stiffly.

"You don't really want to do that," Domino says.

"I do."

"You don't." They stretch their arms up over their head,

languid. "I can tell when you want something. You soak yourself with your own perfume. When you're eager and ready and dripping—I can taste it on the air, Kinsey. Everyone can. So sweet." They lick their lips, their eyes falling to her beltline, their voice going flat. "But I can't taste you right now. That needle doesn't excite you at all."

"Don't let them get to you," Mads says in her ear.

"Shut up," Kinsey snaps. Domino's head tilts to the side—they thought that was for them—and Kinsey decides to run with it. To let them think she's shutting them down. "Of course it excites me," she tells them, picking up the syringe and giving Domino a dry stare. "Didn't you know that about me? I drench my panties every time I think of performing a core needle biopsy on one of my colleagues."

Domino doesn't seem even a little bit chastised by this. They look her over, considering. "Really?"

Kinsey huffs out a laugh. "Oh, yeah. Nothing gets me hotter than the idea of jamming a needle into you and yanking out some of your tissue. And smearing the sample onto a slide?" She pretends to fan herself with one gloved hand. "Don't get me started."

Domino gives a slow nod, their mouth spreading again into that too-wide grin. Only two canines on each side this time. "Okay. Let's do it, then. But I have a condition."

"That much is obvious."

"No, I mean—I have terms. You have to do something for me if I'm going to do something for you."

Something has been picking at the edges of Kinsey's thoughts for the past couple of hours. It's a thought Jacques already put voice to, and now is the moment it chooses to assert itself in her mind as loud as a scream: *this isn't Domino*. She could have chalked everything else up to them acting strange, feeling sick, having some kind of previously undiscovered illness. But there's nothing in the world that would make the Domino she knows fail to laugh at a stupid joke like the one she just made.

Whoever—whatever—is lying in front of her, it's deadly serious about the demand it wants to make. And it's not her colleague.

"What are your terms?" she asks, and even she can hear the chilliness in her own voice.

"You have to talk me through what you're doing," they say. "Slowly."

She waits for them to add more. When they don't, she shrugs. "Okay."

They grin, give a sinuous little writhe. "Take whatever you want."

Mads becomes brisk after that. "Great. We've got consent. Let's get this over with. Open a fresh swab, the one you opened a second ago has probably dried out by now. And try to stop touching everything, would you?"

Kinsey tries to see the person on the lab table in front of her as just another specimen. She imagines that she's explaining her actions to a student, a grad student maybe, who needs to learn the process. "I'm going to sterilize the surface of the skin with alcohol." She reaches for Domino with a fresh square of damp cotton. She's not sure where to start—they don't have eyes or mouths on their body anymore, and she isn't totally confident that she remembers where those things were located before.

Domino notices her hesitation, points to their armpit. "I'll always show you where to take what you want from me," they whisper, their gaze locked onto her.

Kinsey swabs the area, uncomfortably grateful for the guidance. The building shivers around her again, and this time it doesn't stop.

The wind isn't coming in gusts anymore. The storm is here in earnest.

It's only on the second pass with the swab that she notices something odd. There's no hair in their armpit. Domino usually shaves their body hair, which is why Kinsey didn't notice anything strange at first. But now, upon closer inspection, she realizes: there are no razor bumps, no stubble. There are no creases. Domino's underarm is as smooth as a doll's.

"I'm going to let the alcohol dry a little," she says a little too loudly. "Then I'll insert the needle, uh—"

"You're doing great," Mads murmurs through the earpiece. "You'll put the needle in by about a half inch, then take it out again, easy peasy. If you'd listened to me about getting the supplies for a punch biopsy, we could have—"

"Mads."

"Right. Never mind. Look, you'll just be punching out a sample for us to look at. Like taking a core sample from a tree. Or maybe more like a hole punch, at that depth. Don't say hole punch, though, it'll freak them out."

Kinsey nods to show them she's got it. "I'll insert the needle, then remove it again. Like a tree." Her voice is shaking. She clears her throat. "Like taking a core sample from a tree. Okay?"

"What are you doing?" Domino asks.

Kinsey freezes. "I'm taking tissue samples, so we can—"

They reach out and touch her wrist. Gentle. Solicitous. "No, I mean—look. I know I've come on strong. Maybe I'm still over the line. But—" They study her face with wide, worried eyes. "I only want this if you want it. If you're sure. You don't seem sure. You seem nervous. Are you nervous?"

Of course she's nervous. She's about to jam a needle

into her coworker's armpit. But she shakes her head. "Not nervous," she says in a low voice. "Excited."

"You're sure?"

She can't bring herself to say yes, so she just nods instead.

"Okay." Domino reaches up with their opposite hand, gently takes her wrist. "If it's just nerves, that's fine. I can help. Let's do it together."

She lets them guide her. They go slowly, their eyes flicking back and forth between Kinsey's eyes and her hand in theirs. They pull her wrist toward their underarm, pausing only when the tip of the needle is just barely denting the skin.

"Are you ready?" they ask. The lights flicker overhead as the wind outside picks up, a little at a time, hitting faster and harder every few seconds.

All Kinsey can feel—all she can think about—is the feel of their fingers on her wrist. She takes a deep breath, then nods.

Domino pulls on her wrist, angling the needle up toward their collarbone. She lets her arm move with them, sliding the needle into the taut skin of their too-smooth armpit. They don't flinch, but they do draw in a slow, steady breath. Their chest expands on the inhale, seems to engulf the needle.

"Wait," Kinsey says. "Wait, don't breathe so deep. I don't want to go in too far, Mads said I could hit an artery if I'm not careful."

"I want you to go in farther," Domino whispers. "I want to take you deeper."

"Kinsey?" Mads asks through the earpiece. "What's going on? Can you move so I can see Domino? Remember what I said about the axillary artery, you really don't want to hit that."

Kinsey realizes that she's got her back to the observation window. She tries to shuffle to one side, but Domino holds her wrist tight. "Don't go," they breathe. "Give me more."

"I can't," Kinsey says. "I'll hurt you."

"I told you, you can't hurt me." They tug on her wrist again. She doesn't have time to react, to resist—her hand surges toward them, and the needle plunges deeper, until it's in them all the way to the hilt. Domino pushes her hand away again, letting the needle emerge by a full inch before pulling her back in. "Like that." They sigh as the needle plunges back into them.

Kinsey jerks her hand away, stumbles backward. "What—what are you—no," she stammers.

"Kinsey? Kinsey, what's happening?" Mads is borderline frantic in her ear. "Are you okay?"

"I thought you liked it," Domino says. Slowly, so slowly, they pull the needle out. A high, breathy moan slips between their lips as the point of the needle emerges. A thin trickle of sand follows it, streaming out of a peppercorn-sized hole in their skin. "Will you tell me what I'm doing wrong?"

"All of this is wrong," Kinsey breathes, her stomach clenching at the sight of that sand. The lights flicker again. "Where is that sand coming from? What's—what's happening to you?"

"Kinsey," Mads says urgently. "Talk to me."

Kinsey pulls the earpiece out and tucks it into her pocket. She doesn't think about why. She can't seem to think about anything. Her heart hammers in her ears as she stares at that small black hole in Domino's body.

Domino stares at Kinsey intently, their face a mask of

concentration. "I didn't get it quite right, did I?" they say at last. "You don't like me yet. That's okay. I think I see the problem. I can fix it."

After a moment, the hole in their underarm begins to widen.

"Domino?" Kinsey breathes. "What's happening to—"

"Shhh." A few grains of sand make their way down Domino's temple. Kinsey feels an answering bead of sweat at the small of her back. "Just give me a second."

As Kinsey watches, the hole grows until it's the size of a bottlecap. There's still no blood—just pulsing red darkness, damp invitation. The skin around the hole ripples, then puckers up to form two neat parentheses of pink flesh. Domino shifts their weight on the lab table and as they move, the skin of their underarm rucks up like a lifted skirt, folds forming over and around each other, sliding across each other, crumpling like a fistful of satin before smoothing out again.

"Wait," she breathes, just as a small tender node of raw pink pushes its way up out of Domino's skin at the apex of the cluster of folds. She has to hold back the rest of the sentence: *for me*.

"Is that better?" Domino asks, reaching across their own chest to trace a finger along the brand-new orifice nestled in the crook where their shoulder meets their ribcage. At the brush of their finger, Kinsey catches the faintest glisten of moisture.

Her mouth floods with saliva. She doesn't understand what she's seeing, doesn't understand what she's feeling. She wants this to stop. She needs it to continue. She licks her lips and she tastes something sweet and floral on the air, something familiar, something that reminds her of pulsing muscle gripping her thumb and forefinger.

Domino twists their head to smirk up at her, still caressing themselves. Spreading themselves, just for her. They keep their eyes locked on her as they slide a finger inside the slick hole in their underarm. Kinsey is still holding the syringe in one hand. She feels her other hand rising of its own accord, reaching toward the dewdrop of moisture that's seeping up around the edges of the hole. She's going to touch Domino, she's going to feel what they feel, she's going to slip the tip of her tongue between those satiny folds and—

"Kinsey!" The door to the exam room opens with a bang. Kinsey whips around to see Mads standing in the doorway, their face stark with fear. "Are you okay?"

"I'm fine," Kinsey says weakly. "It's—we were just—"

"She was just getting that tissue sample," Domino says. Kinsey looks back to see them lying with their arms at their sides, their hands folded neatly across their belly. The syringe is on the lab tray next to the discarded alcohol pad. Nothing looks out of the ordinary.

Kinsey can still taste Domino on the air. She bites her lips to keep from licking them.

She picks up the syringe, turns on her heel, and walks to the door. She hands the syringe to Mads as she passes them. "That should be enough," she says brusquely. She knows she should clean up after herself. She knows she should tell Mads what she just saw. She knows a lot of things. But at the moment, she doesn't care about what she knows.

Kinsey goes to her bunk. The wind on the other side of the back wall of her room is just picking up into a feral, wolf-like howl. She ignores it. She ignores everything. She locks the door and pulls the painting off the wall. The photo taped to the back flutters free, the stickiness of the tape nearly spent.

She doesn't put it back until the next morning.

Saskia shades her eyes with the flat of one hand. The sun is tyrannical today, lashing the entire team with whipcrack heat. The air around them is still as a hiding hare, not offering even a sour breath of relief.

"I think we should go inside," she says evenly. "For at least a few hours."

Kinsey looks up from the grid she's laying out across the sand. "We haven't even started taking samples yet. Domino, are you done with the scissors?"

Domino slowly cuts a length of twine, then hands the scissors over. Their arms move strangely, like they're reaching through water.

Saskia points at them. "Domino is lightheaded. And Kinsey, you're not sweating at all. Nkrumah hasn't stood upright in half an hour. And Jacques . . ." She glances over at Jacques. "I don't actually know. He doesn't look different from normal, but—"

"We get it," Jacques grumbles. "I'm fine, okay? I'm just tired."

"We should go inside," Saskia says again. She thumbs the necklace that hangs at her throat. "Water. Shade. Little recovery. What do you say?"

Kinsey looks around at her team and sees the way they all sag under the punishing weight of the heat. She grudgingly rises, feels the blood in her legs unpool, watches as the horizon swims and shimmers in the distance. "One hour," she says. "Unless Mads says we need longer. Which they won't. Deal?"

Saskia's already gone, striding back the way they'd come at dawn. As soon as Kinsey starts walking, she knows that Saskia was right—she can feel the full breadth of the kilometer between them and the station, the way it stretches relentlessly between her team and the respite they all clearly need. She stumbles over her own feet, kicking up dust and nearly sprawling across a trail of carpenter ants.

She stands there, trying to recover, waiting for her head to stop spinning. She startles at the feel of a cool, dry hand on her elbow. "Come on, then," Saskia says in a low voice, her lips curling up at the corners. "I'm sure Mads will say I was being silly and inefficient, making us go back. Let's go talk to them, so you can say you told me so."

They walk together, Saskia clearly slowing her pace to stay beside Kinsey. She points at things as they pass—things that are mundane to the desert, but still at least a little incredible to everyone on the team. A massive lizard resting in the shade of a stone, and his smaller counterpart basking in the sun up above, both of them watching the passersby with suspicious, darting eyes. A thorny bush so covered in caterpillar webbing that it looks like a fresh-spun cone of cotton candy. A black seam in a rockface that sets off a debate about whether it would make sense for there to be coal out here. Saskia gets them talking, checks in on each of them subtly enough that they don't snap at her.

When they get back to the station, she stands by graciously as Mads berates the entire team for staying in the field during the hottest part of the day. Kinsey finds her twenty minutes later, after a steady stream of water and cool damp compresses have brought her most of the way back to herself.

"You have every right to say that you told me so. That was stupid," Kinsey says evenly. "I could have gotten us killed."

Saskia shakes her head and offers Kinsey a small, conspiratorial smile. "No way. I remember when you interviewed me, Kinsey. You told me that you need every person on your team to be ready to put you in a headlock and drag you out of the field."

Kinsey doesn't feel the warmth rising in her cheeks, but she knows it's there, joining the flush of her lingering heat exhaustion. "I didn't think I'd need—"

"Sure you did." Saskia gives a liquid shrug. "So you see? You have nothing to apologize for. You couldn't have gotten us killed. We'd never let you do such a thing. You made sure of it when you brought us on."

"Still, though, I'm—"

"You're perspiring again. Good sign." She grins, eyeing Kinsey's hairline. "Come on. Let's go show Mads. They'll be thrilled to see it. Mads! Kinsey's sweaty!"

She leads the way to the exam room, and Kinsey follows.

Kinsey wakes in the morning to the sound of Mads pacing in the hall outside her door. She doesn't know how early it is. She doesn't have a window in her bedroom, doesn't have a bedside clock, hasn't charged her cell phone in months. Here at the station, she gets up when Mads gets up—their footfalls are her morning alarm. It could be midnight. It could be noon. All she knows is that the wind outside is still hammering at her wall, and Mads is up, so she is up.

She opens the bedroom door and pokes her head out. "What time is it? Is that storm still going? Did you figure out how to read Weatherman?"

Mads, who had just finished stomping past her door, whips around. Their face is wild with relief. "Oh, good, you're awake." They hand her an unopened packet of wild berry Toaster Strudel. "There's breakfast. Come with me."

Kinsey, still in the tank top and underwear she slept in, stumbles down the dim hallway after them. The research station is strange with the lights off. Liminal. It feels like a bus station, or a movie set, or a shopping mall after all the stores have closed for the day. "Where are we going?" she asks, her voice still thick with sleep.

"Lab," Mads answers. "Storm's been going all night. Hell out there." Kinsey frowns. Mads isn't usually this short with her. Mads isn't usually short with anyone. They're not a huge talker, but they're also perma-calm, existing in a state of enormous sanguinity. Before they burst into the exam room the other day, she's never seen them so much as shout. Now, they're curt and hurried, stalking toward the lab like they've got a pot boiling in there.

As they hustle past the exam room, Kinsey notices that someone has taped cardboard over the window. There's more duct tape on the door than there was when she sealed Domino inside the day before, too—a lot more. So much that the door itself is no longer visible.

"Is Domino still in there?" she whispers.

Mads doesn't answer. They keep moving, down the hall and through the open door of the lab, ignoring the whine of the wind on the other side of the exterior wall. She realizes that Mads is still wearing the clothes they had on yesterday. She wonders if they've slept at all.

The lab itself isn't substantially different from the canteen, with the food swapped out for equipment and tech. Wire shelves line the walls. Stainless steel lab tables stand in two rows in the center of the room. They're on rubber-footed legs instead of locking casters, built for stability instead of mobility, but otherwise there's no discernible difference between them and the exam table in the room next door.

Weatherman stands in one corner, looking for all the

world like an arcade game. The big glass screen shows a stream of incoming storm data in shades of red and green and amber. It fills the lab with a flickering glow. Kinsey watches the flow of numbers and coordinates, wishing she'd done more than a cursory training session. She knows the numbers indicate danger, but she has no idea how much danger she and her team might actually be in.

One of the lab tables is littered with the detritus of a long night's work: crumpled paper towels, discarded pipettes and wadded nitrile gloves, paraffin wax on a cordless warmer, hydrogen peroxide, dye, droppers, formalin in a dark brown glass bottle, a jug of ethanol with *Jacques don't drink me!* scribbled on a stripe of masking tape across the front. The other table is bare, with the exception of two compound microscopes and a lab notebook.

The wind is loud in here. It's on just the other side of the wall, same as in her bedroom. It yanks at the wall like it wants to get inside, banshee-yowl and scouring sand. On the other side of that wall, Kinsey knows the sky is either pitch-black or Hell-red.

Mads hurries to the microscope, ignoring the mess behind them and the noise around them. "While I was in the exam room, after you left—"

"Sorry, by the way," Kinsey interrupts. "I shouldn't have left like that." She's not sure how embarrassed she should be, not sure how much Mads saw. She wonders what Domino told them.

They look up at her and all she sees in their eyes is understanding. "It's fine. I shouldn't have made you collect the sample all on your own. That wasn't fair to you."

"None of this is fair," she responds gently.

Mads looks back to the microscope. "Well," they say, adjusting the focus minutely, "anyway, after you left, I made sure Domino was okay, and I grabbed the tissue sample you took from them. It was a great one. Kind of a lot of tissue, actually. Like . . . way too much. I'm not sure how they weren't seriously injured." They pause for a moment, leaving a gap that Kinsey knows she's supposed to fill with some kind of explanation. She lets the silence hang until Mads continues. "But they seemed fine, so. While I was in the room, I figured I might as well take a tissue sample from the specimen, too."

It takes Kinsey a moment to remember the specimen they found in the desert, the creature that started all the chaos. "That would have been good practice for me before I stabbed Domino in the armpit, huh?"

That draws a short, humorless laugh out of Mads. "You have no idea how right you are. Come look at this." They lean back from the microscope, gesture for her to take their place.

Kinsey peers into the eyepiece. "This doesn't look like a tissue sample," she says. "What is it?"

"That's the sample I took from the specimen," Mads says. "What do you see?"

She glances up at them, surprised. Mads doesn't usually get didactic, isn't one for leading questions or theatre. But she realizes quickly that they're as far from theatrical as a person can get. They don't have the smug *time to teach you something* look that Saskia gets when she's about to make a member of the team play Socratic Seminar with her.

They look scared.

Kinsey studies their expression for a moment. They're reality-testing, she realizes. Just like she did, when she needed the team to tell her that they could see that something was wrong with Domino. Mads needs her to tell them what she sees, so they can be sure of what they think *they* saw.

She looks again. She can feel the shriek of the wind outside in her back teeth. Her eye adjusts slowly to the view through the microscope lens. There's a tangle of branching filaments on the slide. "This looks a lot like a slime mold," she says. "If it went through the dryer by mistake. There's so much overlap in the hyphae. But—*jesus*, it's moving fast." As she watches, the filaments twitch their way out of view, then come back again. "Fungus doesn't move that quick."

"That's what I thought too." Mads sounds a little more grounded now, bordering on excited. "But look. Look at the crossroads."

It takes Kinsey a moment to understand, but then her eyes land on the places where the filaments cross over each other. Pinkish clusters hide at every intersection, tucked into corners and crevices. Kinsey thinks, just for an instant, of Domino's armpit. She steps away from the microscope, trains her eyes on Mads. "Okay," she says. "What is that? Bacteria?"

"Viruses. I think. It's hard to say anything definitively, obviously. But—I think the fungus is trapping droplets of moisture at those intersections, and the virus that got us all sick is hanging out in those droplets."

"You're suggesting, what? The fungus is . . . farming the virus?"

Mads looks at her sidelong. They study her for several seconds before speaking. "You remember how I didn't call you crazy when you said you thought you saw a mouth on Domino's chest?"

"It was four mouths," she says.

"The point is, I listened. Right?" They wait for her to nod. "I'm going to need you to return the favor."

"Just tell me."

"Okay. Okay." They draw a deep breath, shake out their fingers. "Here goes. I think . . . it's a lichen."

Kinsey almost laughs, catches herself at the last second. "What?"

"It's possible."

"No, it's not." She understands now why Mads wanted her here, so she could tell them they're being ridiculous. She's happy to oblige. "Lichen is mutualistic. A virus can't participate in that kind of exchange."

"I think it can, though."

"How? A virus has nothing to bargain with. It only knows how to invade and multiply itself. A lichen needs something to hold structure and something to make energy. The fungus here has structure, sure, but it obviously isn't making energy, and it's not like a virus can photosynthesize. Unless you saw that specimen turn green at some point and I just missed it?"

Mads cracks a smile. "No Incredible Hulk moments in the exam room as far as I'm aware. But—the energy thing? It's not *totally* impossible for the virus to be an active participant in that. I mean, at Aix-Marseille, they found those giant viruses that were making their own energy. And we've seen that they can communicate with each other, and we know that fungi can communicate with, like, anything. There's no reason to think this fungus wouldn't be able to communicate with the virus, maybe exchanging moisture for energy? That weblike structure seems really efficient at trapping water. Out here, there's no better bargaining chip."

Peering through the microscope again, Kinsey can make out movement in those pink clusters. "Those pink things can't be viruses. It's not possible to see a virus with the naked eye," she says.

"This isn't your naked eye," Mads points out. "It's a microscope."

"You know what I mean."

"I do, and you're still wrong. Here." Mads scoots in next to her, increases the magnification by 400x. "Can you see that?"

"Almost. But c'mon, Mads. An optical microscope's usefulness bottoms out at . . . what, two or three hundred nanometers across?" Kinsey makes a few small, halfhearted adjustments to the focus. "Unless you're getting involved with lasers and radiation and shit, which I know TQI isn't sending our way."

"Yeah, three hundred nanometers. Giant viruses are bigger than that. Four, five hundred nanometers, and that's just the ones we already know about."

Kinsey finally gets the resolution right, and in that moment, she stops listening to Mads. Hell, she stops breathing altogether—because Mads is right. She can see them clearly now: giant viruses, easily six hundred nanometers in diameter, clustered together in what looks like a bubble of fluid at the intersection of two strands of fungal hyphae. They look hexagonal from above, but she knows that they're more complex than that—icosahedrons, made up of twenty triangular faces, covered in minuscule filaments that help them find their way through the world.

Rare as precious gems. Massive. Gorgeous.

Kinsey's only ever seen them in pictures, never in real life. Her legs go weak. Her tongue feels heavy in her mouth. She is suddenly very aware that she's in her underwear. The thin cotton doesn't feel like enough of a barrier between her and the cool air of the lab, not now that she's seen this. She shifts her weight from one foot to the other, then stills, not wanting to create any more friction than she already has.

"Do you see it?" Mads asks. They're very close.

"I see it," she whispers. "Yeah. That's a virus, alright." Kinsey thinks of Domino tasting the air, saying that everyone could tell when she wanted something. She presses her thighs together hard.

"So. Okay." Mads seems so absorbed by the possibility of this lichen that Kinsey realizes they probably wouldn't notice if she started rubbing herself against the lab table. "I think we're looking at a new form of lichen," they say. "The fungus forms the structure, kind of a protective skeleton, right? Plus it captures water. And the virus keeps the whole thing mobile, provides some energy. Helps the fungus gain entry."

"Entry?"

"Yeah."

"What does that mean?"

The crackle in the air curdles. "You know what it means. You know what viruses do."

Kinsey does know what viruses do. She forces herself to look away from the sample, meets Mads's eyes. "Lichens grow on surfaces, though. You said you got this sample off the specimen, right? Was it in the hair, or . . . ?"

Mads shakes their head. "This is the tissue sample. I took it from the specimen's thigh, and another one from the back of the neck. They're the same. They both look just like this."

"That can't be right. That would mean this is what the specimen's skin is made of." She looks at Mads urgently. "That can't be right," she says again, more insistent this time.

Mads lifts their shoulders in a high shrug and doesn't lower them. "It is, though. And look at this." They gesture to the second microscope.

Kinsey peers into the eyepiece. "I see what you mean,"

she says, not wanting to admit what she's seeing. "It does look the same. So this is the sample from the neck, then?"

Mads doesn't answer.

"Mads? This is from the neck sample you took off the specimen?"

Still no answer.

Kinsey looks up to see Mads staring at her. Their gaze is hollow, their mouth slack. "No," they say at last. They look like they want to continue, but they don't.

It takes Kinsey a moment to understand, and when she does, she wishes she didn't. She asks a question she knows the answer to, if only to buy herself a few seconds before the truth becomes true—before she learns something she can't back away from. "Is this more of the sample you took from the thigh, then?"

Mads shakes their head again. "Kinsey," they say softly.

"Don't," she says.

But they do.

"That's from Domino," they tell her. "That's from the deepest part of the sample you took. I checked the entire thing, and there was no human tissue *anywhere*. This isn't just contamination. As far as I can tell," they continue, "that's what Domino is made of now."

Kinsey looks back down into the microscope. Her eyes land on the cluster of viruses. A muscle deep within her sex clenches at the sight, even as dread hisses across the surface of her mind. She remembers the strange way she responded to Domino—the irresistible frisson of attraction between them, the way she wasn't able to look away from the deft movements of their fingers. It's the same feeling she has now, looking into this microscope.

She knows that Mads is right. She knows that her instinct from earlier is right, too.

The Domino she knew is gone. And whatever's left—whatever took their place—some part of her recognizes it for what it is.

A virus.

A virus she desperately *wants*.

And it seems to want her right back.

Nkrumah is drunk. So is everyone—Jacques has been pouring a lethal combination of vodka, lemon juice, and grape electrolyte powder into them for hours. But Nkrumah is on the floor, lying on her back, staring up at the ceiling and rambling semi-coherently about desert carrion birds, so she's the one they're all making fun of.

"Shut up," she says through a laugh, waving one finger at the ceiling. "Shut up, none of you are—listen. Listen!"

"We're all listening," Mads says, sitting on one of the couches and dropping their chin into their palms. "Speak, prophet."

"Listen. They are the immune system of the ecosystem!"

Everyone cheers. Saskia punches the air and lets out a shockingly resonant *wooo!*

"We love ecosystems. And immune systems," Domino says, toeing Nkrumah's knee to make her leg wobble.

She bats ineffectively at their foot with one hand. "You don't patronize me. Just because you're good at eating pussy doesn't mean you get to—" The rest of her sentence is drowned out by laughter.

Even Kinsey is cackling. "Wait wait wait," she gasps. "You two? Nkrumah and Domino? You can't be serious!"

Nkrumah pushes herself up onto her elbows and squints at Kinsey. "What's so funny about that? I'm hot. Look at me. I'm hot!"

"Of course you're hot," Jacques says indulgently, sloshing a measure of vibrant purple liquid out of an Erlenmeyer flask that's been repurposed as a pitcher. Most of the drink makes it into Nkrumah's mug. "And Domino's hot. But you don't like it when people try to be funny, and Domino—"

"Is effortlessly funny," Domino finishes. "And great at eating pussy."

Kinsey glances up to see that Saskia is bright pink. She usually flushes when she drinks, but not like this. She drifts out of the canteen a minute later, and Kinsey quietly trails her to the airlock, catching the interior door when Saskia slips through it.

"Where you goin'?" Kinsey whispers into the dark vestibule.

"Just taking a moment." Saskia is just a shadow among shadows, but Kinsey can hear the damp weight of tears in her voice. "I'll be back to the party soon, promise."

". . . is it because of Domino and Nkrumah?"

There's a long silence. A wet sniff. "Not really. It's about Mads."

Kinsey takes a sip from her nearly empty mug. She hadn't

realized she brought it with her, but she's thankful she did. "Mads."

"They're just so discreet. They don't make jokes like the ones Nkrumah and Domino make. And it makes me wonder if—"

"Saskia, hang on a second," Kinsey interrupts carefully. "I need to pee before I can concentrate on this conversation. Is that okay?"

"Oh." Another sniff. "Of course."

Kinsey scans her keycard at the exterior door and walks out into the night. The sky is dusted with stars. Moonlight paints the desert sand in silvery ripples. Kinsey wanders away from the station, listening to the wind as it stirs the world around her. Her heart pounds. She can already feel the hangover she'll have tomorrow.

When she's done, she comes back to find Saskia leaning against the exterior wall of the station.

"I'm fine," Saskia says. "I think I just needed some air."

Kinsey nods. "You and Mads, then?"

"It's nothing. It's just—you know how it is. We've been here for nearly ten months. We were bound to start chewing on each other eventually, right? It's inevitable." She catches herself. "Well. For everyone except you."

"Everyone except me," Kinsey agrees. "You ready to head inside?"

Saskia tilts her head back to rest it against the wall. Her eyes are on the sky. "I'll be there in a minute. I want to find some constellations first."

Kinsey hesitates. She could leave Saskia alone, could go back inside and drink more of Jacques's poison and laugh at Nkrumah. But she's noticed that, over the last ten months, she's chosen to leave Saskia alone a lot. She doesn't want to do it this time.

She leans against the wall next to her colleague, who she realizes she's just starting to think of as a friend. "Mind if I find them with you?"

Saskia smiles up at the sky, her tear-glossed eyes reflecting the bright banner of the Milky Way. "I hoped you would."

Kinsey looks around the lab, meeting each of her team members' eyes as she tells them what she and Mads have discovered. She explains the structure of the lichen. "If you'd like to see it for yourself, Mads brought the microscopes in here for you. So, um."

"So you can sit down after you look," Mads finishes for her. "If you need to."

They take turns looking into the microscopes on the coffee table, one by one. Nkrumah goes last. She takes a long time peering down into the lens. When she returns to her seat on the patched love seat, her gaze remains locked on the microscope, like it might turn to her and speak.

Kinsey continues. "Given how easily the lichen took Domino's shape, and the shape of the specimen we found—we think it can look like anything. Anything living, at least, although I suppose we shouldn't rule out nonliving things as well."

She sees most of her own feelings reflected on their faces. Nkrumah looks focused and interested; her mind will be racing, Kinsey knows, with the scientific possibilities opened up by a mutualistic collaboration between fungus and virus. Nkrumah is always looking for the roads that might unfurl as a result of the team's fieldwork. She's always hoping for broader horizons and brighter futures.

Jacques, meanwhile, is pale and tight-lipped. He's already compartmentalized his grief and heartbreak about Domino. Rather than feeling the weight of loss, he'll be focused on considering the ramifications: the dangers of a fungus that can move with the speed and flexibility of a virus, the horrors of a virus that has the longevity and stability of a fungus. Jacques is the soothsayer of the team, the one who sees trouble on the horizon while everyone else is busy staring at a hole in the ground. He always knows when to be worried. Kinsey can see that he's worried now.

Saskia is tougher to read. That's not unusual. Her face tends toward stillness. She's stroking the Eastern Orthodox cross around her neck with her middle finger, long slow strokes that make Kinsey feel like she shouldn't be watching. Saskia is a thinker. She takes her time, assesses situations slowly, combs through information until it falls in shining waves she can run her fingers through easily. The information Mads and Kinsey have delivered to her today is simple in content and complicated in its ramifications. It'll take time for her to organize it in her mind, but once she has, she'll deliver some scathingly concise answer to everything, something that will make the rest of them wonder how they didn't see it sooner.

Mads looks exhausted. Kinsey guesses they've been

awake for thirty hours, maybe more. They clear their throat, and all the remaining eyes in the room snap to them.

"I, um." They hunch their shoulders, jam their hands in their pockets. "I can't figure out a gentle way to put this. Domino." They stop and don't seem to know how to start again. Their eyes lift to the ceiling, like they're listening to the song of the storm raging outside.

"You can say it," Jacques says. His voice is rough. "Domino is gone."

Nkrumah shoots up out of her chair, her arms crossed over her chest. "No, they're not," she snaps. "Stop it. Just because they have, what, a fungal infection? That doesn't mean they're dead. They're in the exam room right now, probably hungry and thirsty because you idiots haven't brought them any—"

"They're not hungry," Saskia says in a low, even voice. "They didn't ask for anything when Kinsey went in to take the sample from them. Remember?"

"That's right." Jacques rocks forward in his seat, rests his elbows on his knees. "And they didn't join us for breakfast yesterday morning. Neither did you, Kinsey. I guess because you were with them."

She frowns to herself, remembering. "Yeah, I was with them. They wanted to go look at the specimen—at least, that's what they said. I think they just wanted to get me alone, though. We went straight into the lab from the shower. Our hair was still wet. Well," she says, considering, "mine was. Theirs was already dry."

"The fungus would be efficient at trapping and storing moisture," Mads offers. "Maybe it was already distributed throughout the primary body."

"Don't talk about them that way," Nkrumah pleads. "Listen to yourselves. 'The body'? That's not how we talk about our—our colleague." Her voice breaks, her eyes dropping to the floor. Domino's never been just a colleague to Nkrumah, and she's never been good at pretending otherwise.

"It sounds like that's not our *colleague* in there anymore," Jacques says gently. "The sample Kinsey took—"

"Oh, so we're deciding that based off one sample? A sample we got from someone who doesn't even know how to take one properly?"

"I do know how to take a sample," Kinsey replies. "Not in a way that wouldn't hurt a living person, so yeah, Mads was talking me through it. But I didn't get the chance to follow Mads's instructions, because Domino, um. They took the needle from me. They took it, and they pushed it in." She bites back the memory of how much they'd seemed to enjoy the penetration of the wide-bore needle as it slid into the moist cavern of their body. "It went deep. Way too deep. That needle went in far enough that honestly, I was scared it might kill them."

"It probably wouldn't have killed them," Mads says. "Probably. But at the very least it would have hurt. A lot."

"You sound disappointed that you didn't manage to murder them with your incompetence." Nkrumah starts pacing, her arms still crossed, her shoulders taut. "You sound like you want us to abandon them just because they're freaking you out."

Mads lets out an exasperated sigh. "Nobody wants Domino gone. You know that."

"I get what you're saying, though. And I'm sorry." Kinsey makes sure she's facing Nkrumah head-on, looking her square in the eyes. She doesn't want to say what comes next, but more than that, she doesn't want to leave Nkrumah alone with it. "But what I'm telling you is, with how far Domino pushed that needle in, they should have been incapacitated with pain. But they weren't. They didn't seem to notice that it was happening at all. Whatever's going on with their body, they're different now. And not in the way that change is the only constant of biology," she adds, seeing Nkrumah's rebuttal before it comes. "I'm telling you that they're fundamentally transformed on a biological level, and we need to figure out what that means before we can figure out what to do with them."

Nkrumah's shoulders sag. It looks like she's nearing acceptance—but then Jacques weighs in.

"We just need to accept the reality of the situation," he supplies. "We discovered something new. Discovery comes with consequences. Domino would understand that."

Nkrumah looks at him with stark disbelief for a few seconds before turning and walking out of the room. A moment later, there's the beep of the card reader on the interior airlock door, then a second, fainter beep as Nkrumah storms outside.

"She shouldn't be out there," Kinsey says. "It's dangerous."

"She knows the risks. Let her go," Mads says softly.

Kinsey doesn't like it—the idea of a member of her team standing out in the storm. The wind is quieter now, but the sand out there will still be whipping across the desert hard enough to strip the top layer of flesh from anything that stands still for too long. She hopes Nkrumah grabbed eye protection on the way out, at least. "Fucks sake, Jacques. Was that necessary?"

Jacques frowns and mutters, "It's true."

Saskia doesn't make a sound, doesn't move—but somehow, something about her shifts to convey that she's ready to share a thought. Jacques, Mads, and Kinsey all turn to her, attentive.

"What's up?" Kinsey asks.

Saskia doesn't hesitate in her reply. "Do you already know what you're going to do with it? The thing in the exam room, I mean? No? I didn't think so." She says it matter-of-factly. "And what about the rest of us?"

Mads blinks at her, their eyes sharp with the adrenalized alertness that comes on the other side of extreme fatigue. "The rest of us," they say. It's not a question.

Jacques drops his head into his hands. "Fuck. She's right."

Whatever understanding the three of them are sharing, Kinsey's on the outside of it. She's tired, sure—her brain has been fried by several days of near-compulsive masturbation, on top of the shock of what's happened to Domino. She can understand all the reasons for her lack of comprehension and still hate the outcome, especially when the outcome puts her behind the rest of her team.

"Let's not make any assumptions," she says, which is what she always says when she needs someone to explain something to her but doesn't want to ask for clarification.

Saskia gives her a knowing smirk that says *I'm onto you*. It's gone before Kinsey can ask what it's about. "Right," Saskia says slowly. "Well. This lichen went into Domino's body, got them sick, and then—this is the idea, isn't it?—consumed and replaced them?"

"Duplicated them," Mads says. They sound nauseated. "It made a copy. I don't know how that's even possible, but—"

"We don't need to know how it's possible right now," Jacques says. "That's a question for later, when we've got it contained. When we're safe. Right now all that matters for our purposes is that it can happen."

"And we need to make sure it didn't happen to any of

us," Saskia says with an elegant nod. "Because we all got sick, too, which means the lichen probably infected us the same way it infected Domino."

Kinsey's stomach sinks. This is the thing they all understood before she did. It probably came to mind for them right away, she realizes, because they *did* all get sick. Saskia, Mads, Jacques, Nkrumah, and Domino all had the same vomiting, the same coughing, the same fever.

None of them know that it didn't touch her. *I'm different*, she thinks, and the thought has an unwholesome glow to it, a smugness and a certainty that she doesn't want to let herself embrace. She can't help wondering whether the virus passed her over for the same reason it turned Domino's underarm into a wet, fuckable hole. *It likes me.* Warmth climbs her throat, radiates into her cheeks. She covers her face with her hands, tries to look devastated.

When she looks up, Saskia is staring at her. Smiling at her. It's a small, secret smile, a barely there smile. An *I know what you're thinking* smile. *But she can't know*, Kinsey thinks—and then Saskia is looking at Mads and Jacques, her expression returning to its usual calm neutrality. A moment later, Nkrumah comes back coated in dust and announces that she's calmed down, and the moment is so thoroughly gone that Kinsey can't be sure it ever really happened at all.

"Everybody gets a biopsy," Nkrumah announces.

Jacques jumps to his feet. "Absolutely not."

"It's the only way to confirm who's infected." Mads nods at Nkrumah. "I think it's the right call."

"Boss?" Jacques glares at Kinsey. "Tell them we're not doing that. I don't want—"

"Even in a clinical setting," Saskia cuts in before Jacques can finish, "biopsies are risky. If something goes wrong, you could introduce the pathogen into our systems. Why don't we start with a visual inspection first, to see if we can spot any obvious signs of infection?"

Jacques gives a single, decisive nod. "See, that makes sense. That's what my dermatologist does—plays spot-the-differences. The only thing working in our favor right now is the fact that the lichen's not good at this," he adds.

"Oh, *now* you're willing to listen to your dermatologist?" Mads mutters.

"I don't know if I agree that it's 'not good at this,'" Kinsey says thoughtfully, ignoring Mads. "That Domino duplicate was a decent first draft. It was flawed, sure, but that's just because the lichen couldn't have known yet that there's such specificity to the distribution of mouths and eyes on the human body."

Nkrumah pulls Jacques's rum out of the storage closet. The sound of the wind outside howls into the room as she opens the door, gets swallowed up again when she closes it. "Whether it's good or not isn't the point. The point is that it's not *perfect*." She grabs a packet of powdered apple cider mix, studies it, puts it back unopened. "The lichen is still figuring out what goes where. Or maybe it doesn't care what goes where."

"Fine, that works as a starting point. We check to see if we all look like we're supposed to, right?" Mads says. "Nkrumah, there's cocoa mix behind the plates."

"That's not better." She pours a generous amount of rum into a mug and takes a pull. "We should lock down until we know who's who. Nobody leaves the station, nobody goes anywhere alone. We stay in pairs at the very minimum. Sound good?"

"Keycards," Jacques says decisively. "Everybody put them on the table."

Kinsey hesitates. "If we give up our keycards, we won't be able to run away. Unless we prop the airlock doors open, which doesn't feel safe, either. Especially with the sandstorm."

"The sandstorm is starting to chill out. It's red outside, so shouldn't be too long before we've got daylight out there," Nkrumah says, and it's too easy for Kinsey to picture her standing outside in the bloodred whirlwind, screaming into the storm as sand scours her throat. "It's just for now," Nkrumah continues, slapping her keycard down onto the table. Saskia follows suit right away, followed by Jacques and Mads. They all stare at Kinsey until she gingerly sets her own keycard on top of the pile. Nkrumah gives a nod of satisfaction. "Okay. Let's do it. Clothes off."

Kinsey freezes. The others have seen her naked before, sure, but not the same way they've seen each other. They know each other's bodies intimately. Mads knows what Saskia tastes like. Jacques knows how Saskia's thighs feel against the sides of his head. Nkrumah has felt Saskia's throat beneath her palms. Kinsey isn't part of that body of knowledge. For them to see her naked, up-close, intent—that will be new for everyone.

She realizes she's staring at Saskia, wrenches her gaze away. Scolds herself for getting distracted by things that aren't her business. "You heard Nkrumah," she says. "Clothes off. Are we doing this in pairs, or by committee?"

"Pairs," Mads says. "That makes the most sense. Me and Jacques, since we've never been romantic. No emotional conflict of interest to keep us from being honest about what we see, right?"

Jacques holds a hand to his heart in mock outrage. "You wound me, Mads."

Nkrumah clears her throat. "We can't do pairs. There are only five of us."

There's a long silence as everyone realizes Mads's mistake—pairs would have worked perfectly, if Domino was around. But they're not around, and they never will be again.

"I don't want to strip in front of everyone," Saskia finally says. "I'd prefer to be one-on-one with somebody."

Kinsey speaks before she realizes what she's saying. "I'll pair with Saskia. Nkrumah, are you okay being a trio with Mads and Jacques?"

"Wouldn't be the first time," Jacques says, flashing a sudden grin.

Nkrumah frowns. "We shouldn't split up."

"It doesn't count as splitting up if nobody's alone." Mads's tone is so calm and reasonable that Nkrumah's frown falters. "As long as we're all on the same page, right?"

Everyone is silent until Nkrumah nods. "Okay. As long as we're on the same page."

Kinsey is about to head out of the room with Saskia, but pauses. "Make sure you count each other's teeth," she says after a moment. "Look for extras."

Jacques's smile fades. "Will do," he says softly, then drops his head to attend to the button fly on his jeans.

Saskia and Kinsey head out of the canteen and walk to the lab together. Saskia trails her fingers along the wall, humming a low tone in harmony with the song of the storm that rages just a few inches away from her fingertips. "Teeth," she says, dropping the tune. "I wouldn't have thought of that."

"I noticed yesterday. On Domino." Kinsey is determined not to look at the cardboard-covered exam room window as they pass it. "It was subtle, though. I like the way Nkrumah put it—"

"Not a matter of not being good. Just a matter of not being perfect," Saskia finishes. "I liked that too. Seems more respectful. Speaking of respect," she adds, holding the door to the lab open for Kinsey, "I didn't get a chance to tell you, I was very impressed by your work yesterday."

Kinsey steps into the lab, hits the light switch, waits for the fluorescents to slowly flicker to life. Only half of them turn on. In the corner, Weatherman glows with red streams of data. "My work? You mean how I completely botched that sample?"

Saskia closes the door and leans against it. "No. I mean how you manipulated Domino."

"I'm not following you."

"You made them think you were aroused by the idea of taking a biopsy. It was clever. All you had to do was connect the tissue sample to the promise of sex." She's toying with her cross necklace again, sliding the pendant slowly back and forth on the chain. Half her face is tinted red from Weatherman's display. "You exploited that brilliantly."

"Exploited isn't the word I would use," Kinsey says, although she knows it's the right word. "I didn't even do that on purpose. Wait, how did you hear that? Were you on the headset with Mads?"

"They weren't using the headset, just the walkie speaker." Saskia's mouth spreads into a painfully wide smile. "I love the way you took advantage of Domino's desire for you. You used it to make them vulnerable. You could have eaten them alive and they would have thanked you for it, so long as you moaned while you took the first bite."

Kinsey stares at Saskia, counting teeth. There's something she doesn't like about the idea that Mads had her on the walkie's speaker while she was in the exam room. But the longer she looks at Saskia, the harder it is to connect with that discomfort. She finds her eyes lingering on Saskia's long after she's lost the mental thread of their conversation, and in the end she simply turns away, pulling her shirt over her head. "Let's get this over with."

Saskia removes everything except her necklace. Kinsey inspects her closely, tells herself this is no different than checking someone for ticks. Saskia's skin is as smooth as spread butter. There's a mole nestled into the soft down of her armpit hair, another in the crook of her neck. A scar zags down the back of one calf. She attributes it to a childhood accident, a fall from a rooftop. "I should have been hurt worse," she says when Kinsey runs a fingertip across it.

"I'm glad you weren't," Kinsey answers. She cups Saskia's ankle in one hand, lifts her foot, studies the curve of her arch and the plump cushions of her toes. It's hard to look away, she finds. This might be the most beautiful foot she's ever seen.

Saskia reaches down, runs her fingers through Kinsey's short hair. "What's the verdict? Am I good, or am I perfect?"

Kinsey looks up. Saskia is staring down at her with that same knowing smirk from before, that look that says *I know what you're thinking*. But she can't know what Kinsey is thinking, because in that moment, Kinsey can't seem to form a single thought. She's never considered that Saskia is beautiful before, except maybe in the abstract, the way she generally appreciates the loveliness of a bird or a rare fossil. But now, on her knees, on top of her folded-up sweatshirt in the middle of the lab, she's finally seeing clearly.

"Perfect," Kinsey whispers.

Saskia grins again, wide enough to show off her flawless molars. She helps Kinsey to her feet. "My turn," she says. "Close your eyes."

"Wait, why—"

"So you can't intimidate me. I won't have you taking advantage of me the way you did with Domino," she teases. "Go on. Close them."

Kinsey obeys. She's facing Weatherman, and the darkness behind her eyelids flickers red from the light of the display. She can feel her heartbeat hammering hard in her chest. She jumps at the touch of Saskia's hands on her shoulders.

"So nervous," Saskia purrs. "Are *you* the monster?"

"No." Kinsey laughs. It sounds nervous even to her own ears. "No, but check anyway."

Saskia's fingers skate across Kinsey's shoulders, trace their way down her arms, turn her hands over and caress the insides of her wrists. "Your hands are shaking. Do you need some of Jacques's rum?"

Kinsey doesn't answer. She feels feverish. Her skin is so sensitive that she can feel Saskia's breath stirring the air in front of her, can feel the shift in temperature when Saskia comes closer for a more minute inspection. Cool fingers lace between hers, tug her hand upward.

"You have a birthmark on your palm," Saskia whispers, and Kinsey could swear that she feels lips moving just nanometers from her wrist. "Are you a vampire?"

"Do vampires have birthmarks on their palms?" Kinsey asks, startled enough that she almost opens her eyes.

"How should I know? I'm not a vampire." Saskia allows Kinsey's hands to fall to her sides. She takes Kinsey by the shoulders again, turns her around. Her hands on the back of Kinsey's neck elicit a sudden shiver. "Are you cold?"

The entire building shakes as the wind slaps a firm palm against the broad side of the research station. "No."

"Mmm. You're such a mystery. What's this?" Saskia

rests her palm against the swell of Kinsey's hip on the left side. "You have a bruise."

It takes a moment to remember. "From the exam table," she says. "I ran into it when Domino cornered me in the exam room. It's funny, I didn't even feel it, but it must have left a hell of a mark."

"A hell of a mark," Saskia agrees softly. She gives Kinsey's hip a gentle squeeze, as if she's reluctant to let it go. "I'm sorry that happened, Kinsey."

Kinsey shrugs. "It's okay. It wasn't really Domino, you know?"

"Still." Her hands travel again, tracing a path across Kinsey's belly. Her breath is warm on the back of Kinsey's neck. "It shouldn't have happened like that."

Eyes still closed, Kinsey turns her head as far as she can, until she feels Saskia's lips brushing the cusp of her ear. "What are you doing back there? You're not going to be able to see if you're behind me," Kinsey murmurs, her voice rough.

"I can see everything I need to see," Saskia replies. Her arms are around Kinsey's waist. The skin of them is velvet as her hands dip lower on Kinsey's belly, trailing gooseflesh behind them. "You and I both know you're still Kinsey."

"And you're—Saskia," Kinsey says, the name gasping out of her as she feels the sudden crush of breasts against her back, the slip of a thigh pushing between hers from behind, the chill of Saskia's necklace at the nape of her neck. "What are you—"

"Shhh." Saskia's fingers shift lower still, impossibly soft, impossibly cold.

Kinsey's heart is in her throat. Her skin is on fire. Need floods her, fills her from the bottom up, starting right where Saskia's fingertips are just brushing the coarse hair between her thighs.

She doesn't fight it. A feverish buzz dizzies her entire body. The feeling takes her. She lets it happen, tipping over into thoughtless, wordless need. She shifts her weight, leans back into Saskia's chest, tilts her head to expose her neck in hopes of Saskia's lips and teeth finding their way to the tender flesh there, raises her hips, eager, shameless.

Saskia pours a whispered *yes yes yes* into the cup of Kinsey's ear. She presses in close, her tongue tracing a line down the side of Kinsey's neck. Her fingers sink into the softest part of Kinsey's belly, leaving a cool trail of something damp behind them, a slow drift of sand falling between Kinsey's thighs as they find their way home—

Kinsey's eyes snap open, her arousal congealing into dread. Saskia freezes at the sudden tension that thrums through Kinsey's body. "Wait," Saskia says, but Kinsey doesn't wait, because it's already too late. She already knows the truth. She just has to look down to confirm what she can feel.

Saskia's hands are still where they were resting just a moment before. One cups the small swell of Kinsey's belly; the other is nestled in her pubic hair, a mere breath away from her undoing.

The one on Kinsey's belly looks just like Saskia's hands are supposed to look: slim, pale, nails bitten to the quick.

"I should have known sooner," Kinsey says, closing her eyes. "I should have known the second I started thinking about what it was like for Jacques to fuck you. I don't have those thoughts. Not about you."

"It's okay," Saskia says, her lips against Kinsey's shoulder. A few grains of sand slip down over Kinsey's collarbone.

"Just ignore it. It doesn't have to be a problem if we don't make it a problem."

The hand that rests at the cusp of Kinsey's sex shifts. Kinsey lets out an involuntary whine at the damp pressure it exerts so close to the core of her desire. She can't deny what she feels—she wants this. Her body wants this so much she could scream.

But she also can't deny what she sees. She forces herself to open her eyes again, to look at the thing she's struggling so hard to resist.

Saskia's right hand no longer has the slender, clever fingers that traced their way across Kinsey's shoulders, down her back, over her hips. There's still a wrist, still a palm—but that palm doesn't terminate, doesn't split into five independent digits. Instead, it stretches into a thick rope of muscle, slick and pink, knotted with veins and tendons.

As Kinsey stares, Saskia turns her hand over, showing Kinsey the rest. On the side where Saskia would normally have fingerprints, there's an expanse of wet, bumpy flesh, divided down the center by a faint line. It flexes as Kinsey watches, lithe and supple, questing, tasting. Promising.

"You made a tongue." She makes herself say it out loud. "Your hand has a tongue."

Saskia turns the hand back over, so Kinsey can see the underside of the tongue. "I know," she says. "You were supposed to keep your eyes closed. Tongues aren't nice to look at." There's a smile in her voice. "But they feel good, don't they? Let me taste you, Kinsey."

With all the will she possesses, Kinsey takes a step forward, out of Saskia's arms. "I can't."

Saskia takes a step too, wraps herself around Kinsey tighter than before. "You can." She covers Kinsey's eyes with the hand that has fingers, reaches around to let the tongue trace a circle around one of Kinsey's nipples. Without the heat of a mouth to warm it, the tongue is cold. It leaves a wet trail of chilled spit behind to pinch at Kinsey's breast. Saskia clutches Kinsey close, grinds against her, bites down on her earlobe—it's overwhelming, too much all at once, and Kinsey can't help letting out a throaty moan. "That's better," Saskia breathes. "Just don't look. It's better if you don't look. I understand that now. I made a mistake with Domino, but now I know—"

That name is what finally snaps Kinsey back to herself. She jerks away from Saskia—from the thing that's pretending to be Saskia, she reminds herself like a slap to the face—and bolts for the door.

"Wait—"

"No," Kinsey says, scooping up her clothes as she skids across the lab on bare feet, sand crunching under her heels, red light at her back. She doesn't look behind her because she knows that if she does, she won't be able to resist whatever she sees. "No, you killed Domino, you—you killed Saskia—"

"Wait!!" The lichen yells with Saskia's voice, chases Kinsey with Saskia's feet. It's fast—easily as fast as Kinsey, maybe faster. But this rejection has taken it by surprise. Kinsey's out the door before it's halfway across the lab.

She slams the door shut behind her and leans her full weight against it, panting, clutching her clothes to her chest, staring at the wall that still screams with a smothering wind that's pressing dunes of sand against the base with every passing moment. She can't decide if she hates herself for nearly giving in, or if she hates herself for missing her chance. Her skin puckers in the chill of the hallway. *It's not a problem if we don't make it a problem*, Saskia had said.

It made so much sense when she said it. And now

Kinsey has confirmation of what she suspected before: the virus wants her. It sees her, exactly the way she sees it, and it wants to be with her.

The door at Kinsey's back doesn't have an exterior lock. The handle rattles, the door shoves against her back hard. Saskia—the creature—wants out. It takes all Kinsey's strength to keep it trapped inside. It takes all her will not to dive back into that room with it.

She knows better than to trust herself to resist it. She screams for help, competing with the wind outside. She hopes her team hears her and comes to her rescue—and just as powerfully, she hopes the thing inside the lab will break the door down, pin her to the floor of the hallway, and push that long ropy tongue into her as deep as it can go. She screams, pressing her thighs together to stop herself from dripping with need. She screams and screams and screams.

It's only once Mads arrives that she realizes she's been screaming Saskia's name.

It's too cold outside at night for a picnic to make any sense, but everyone comes out with Mads anyway. They spread out four of Saskia's knitted blankets on the sand a quarter mile from the station.

Domino brings the big pot from the canteen; when they take off the lid, a cloud of steam rises into the air. It's a dish Domino calls Big Noodle, a combination of seven different flavors of instant ramen with a whole bag of frozen vegetables thrown in during the boil. It smells like shrimp and chicken and beef all at once. The tiny cubes of soft carrot stand out against the salt slap of the noodles. Everyone eats out of the pot at once, their forks diving past each other like swooping vultures. No one speaks.

Then Kinsey opens a bottle of wine and hands it to Mads. They look down at it in silence for a minute or two, their hand engulfing the narrow glass neck. Then they raise it high into the air.

"Five years ago," they begin. Their voice is quiet, but the entire desert is so still tonight that it seems like the ear of the world is pressed to Mads's sternum. "Five years ago tonight, I lost track of time. I was at my practice, catching up on paperwork and fucking around on my phone and just kind of . . . I don't know. Probably watching videos or some shit. And when I finally got home, the only person there was this young cop. He was waiting for me on the porch. He looked, I don't know, maybe eighteen?" They look out across the dark desert. "He looked scared to tell me what he had to tell me. I remember thinking, *I can't believe they sent you to do this alone.*"

Saskia reaches out and rests a hand on Mads's shoulder. They reach up and press their palm over her knuckles, hard enough that Kinsey can't tell if they're holding her in place or pushing her away.

"And then he told me what he had to tell me. He gave me the alone-ness. He'd been there alone, and then he handed it off to me, and suddenly, I was the one who was alone. And he went back to wherever baby cops go, and I stayed on my front porch and watched the stars come out, because I couldn't make myself go inside and see how alone I was," Mads says.

They raise the wine bottle high overhead, then take a long drink from it. They cough a few times. "I don't feel that way here. I don't get a moment's fucking peace from any of you," they add, laughing. And then they raise the bottle high again. "Thank you all for not making me be alone out here tonight."

They drink again, then pass the bottle. Mads will stay out here in the cold until the sun comes up, and everyone will stay with them.

Mads drapes a blanket around Kinsey's shoulders. She's on the couch in the little nook outside the exam room. She can't stop shivering. The rest of the team heard her screams and came to her rescue—Mads held the exam room door shut while Jacques and Nkrumah moved bookshelves to form a makeshift barricade. While they did that, Kinsey got dressed, and the entire time, she listened to the sound of Saskia calling her name from within the lab.

Even though she ran—even though she called for help and got it, even though she's shaking with fear—she can't help the yearning that's blooming just beneath the surface of her skin. Everything she's ever wanted is behind two thin walls on either side of her. Domino in the exam room, Saskia in the lab. Everything in her is taut with desire.

She bites the inside of her cheek hard, grips the knitted

blanket in one fist. Forces herself to think of the cost of getting what she wants. Two of her colleagues are dead. Two of her friends. Nothing, she tells herself, could fuck her well enough to make that acceptable.

"So," Mads says, tucking the blanket around Kinsey a little tighter.

"So," she replies. "Saskia's the same as Domino. She had a tongue on her hand."

"A what?"

"A tongue," she repeats. "Instead of fingers."

Mads goes quiet. When Kinsey looks over, she catches them frowning down at their own fingers, flexing the knuckles. She's about to offer to check their thumb for tastebuds when the wind outside suddenly dies.

The quiet that falls is as jarring as the howling that's been surrounding the base for the past several hours. Mads and Kinsey and Jacques all look up at the ceiling, the same way they do when the wind begins. They're all waiting for the other shoe to drop—for the wind to pick back up, twice as loud, or for a thunderclap to announce that a lightning storm is splitting the dust storm open like a wedge splitting a seam into a mountainside.

"Fuck," Nkrumah whispers. "If she's infected, that means we can't go into the lab."

"Not like we've got samples to study anyway," Mads says.

Nkrumah's eyes flash. She rarely loses her temper with Mads, but she looks to be on the verge of it now. "No. But Weatherman's in there."

"We can't read it without Domino," Kinsey offers.

"We could learn," Nkrumah snaps. "We could reread the fucking manual. Without it, we have no way of knowing what's coming for us."

Jacques shrugs. "Okay. So we go in and get Saskia and we toss her in the exam room with Domino. Problem solved."

Mads shakes their head. "Hang on. No way. We can't let her—it, we can't let *it* out of there. It's too dangerous."

"We can handle it." Jacques moves toward the bookshelf barricade. "I'm with Nkrumah. I want access to Weatherman."

"Since when do you agree with me that fast?" Nkrumah's eyes narrow. "Actually . . . since when do you agree with me *ever*?"

Jacques is already trying to budge one of the heavy bookshelves. "I agree with you all the time. And you're right. We need to be able to see what's coming for us. So let's—"

Nkrumah cuts him off. "Hang on a second. Jacques, hold out your arms."

"What?" Jacques looks down at himself, then turns and looks over his shoulder, his eyes wide. "I don't see anything."

"Where is it?" Nkrumah asks. "Show us."

Kinsey is on her feet, the blanket falling away. "What is it?"

"I don't know," Jacques says, looking down at himself. "I don't know, I don't see anything—"

"Bullshit." Nkrumah slowly shakes her head. Her fingers curl and flex at her sides. "You're one of them. You think you're slick, but I see you."

Jacques holds his hands up, palms out. "I didn't do anything. I was just helping move the shelf so we can get Saskia and—"

Nkrumah lifts one hand to point a rigid finger at him. "I see you. I see you, whatever the fuck you are," she says, the pitch of her voice starting to rise. Her every word echoes in the corridor now that there are no bookshelves to soften the sound and no wind to smother it.

Mads steps toward her. "You're tired. We're all tired. Let's not panic and start accusing each other of—"

"I'm not panicked," Nkrumah says. Her index finger aims at Mads and they freeze in place. "Don't come near me. Don't take another step."

Kinsey rises and moves between them, holds a hand out in either direction. "Both of you stop. Nkrumah, go stand with Mads."

"Don't tell me—"

"Now," Kinsey snaps. Without waiting to see if Nkrumah is still refusing to go, she turns to Jacques. He has two arms as far as she can tell. Ten fingers, one crooked from a bad break. "Smile," Kinsey orders, and he does, revealing slightly crooked teeth, one chipped canine, a bouquet of crinkles around each eye. "Turn," she says, and he turns, his arms out by his sides, his feet moving in a slow shuffle.

"He looks normal," Mads says.

"So did Saskia," Nkrumah replies. Kinsey glances over her shoulder to find that Mads has moved closer to Nkrumah, so they're standing together even though Nkrumah hasn't budged. "He's not acting normal. I'm telling you, he's one of those things. We have to—" She stops abruptly midsentence.

Jacques's eyes widen in alarm. "Have to what? Kill me?"

"Of course not," Mads says.

"Probably," Nkrumah says at the same time.

"Wait," Jacques says. "You wouldn't do that. You didn't even kill Domino, and we know for sure that they're infected."

Nkrumah covers her mouth with one hand, seems to chew on a thought for a few seconds. When she drops her hand, her jaw is taut, her eyes glassy. "Not infected," she says. "Dead. You're the one who said I have to accept that it isn't Domino in there anymore, remember? It's something else, it's a—a *lichen*. It's not our friend. All it wants to do is consume us." Her voice wobbles on the last few words and she stops speaking altogether.

"Well, I don't wanna consume anyone, so maybe we can all just calm down. Okay? Okay. Okay?" Jacques is starting to sound genuinely scared. Kinsey doesn't blame him. She's never seen Nkrumah cry. She doesn't want to know what thought is so unbearable that it's brought her colleague to the edge of tears.

She bites her tongue. She can think of something the lichen seems to want, something that Nkrumah doesn't know about. She can't tell her team—can't imagine how she'd even start. But it gives her an idea.

She turns to regard Jacques. Locks her eyes onto his. Wets her lips. "Jacques," she says softly, almost under her breath, hoping that only he can hear. "What do you want?"

He looks at her with stark incomprehension. "What?"

"What do you want?" she asks again. Takes a step toward him. She tries to look at him the way she looked at Domino, the way she looked at Saskia. "You can tell me."

"I—I don't know," he says, shaking his head, his eyes filling with bewildered tears. "I don't know. What do you mean?"

"I mean," she says in a whisper so soft she can barely hear herself, "do you want me?" She's asking him but she's also asking herself: *Do I want him?* Kinsey has never looked at Jacques with desire, nothing even close to it, but she looks at him now and tries to call it up: the way she'd been unable to take her eyes off Domino, the way she'd been unable to resist Saskia's touch. Looking at Jacques, Kinsey tries to see the virus in him, the same way she saw it in them.

Jacques gives his head a fractional shake, more like an involuntary twitch than an expression of preference. "I don't want anything right now. Except maybe a drink," he adds with a half laugh.

Kinsey stares at him for a few more seconds. "He's not infected," she calls over her shoulder, not taking her eyes off Jacques.

"How do you know?" Mads sounds genuinely curious.

"I . . . can tell," Kinsey replies. "Domino and Saskia both made me feel a certain way. Jacques doesn't."

Mads looks at her exactly the way she deserves to be looked at for saying something like that.

Nkrumah shakes her head, unconvinced. "I don't buy it. We can't take one person's word for this. If you're infected, you could be covering for him."

"Oh, but we can take one person's word that I *am* infected?" Jacques says icily, leaning around Kinsey to glare at Nkrumah.

"It doesn't matter either way," Mads insists. "We're not killing Jacques. Not if we're not completely sure."

Nkrumah folds her arms across her chest, tilts her head. On her, this posture is a rattling tail, Kinsey knows. It's a red-dawn sky, a cocked pistol. It's a warning. "Well," she says, "fine."

"Fine?" Jacques whispers.

Nkrumah nods. "We won't kill him."

Ten minutes later, Jacques stands in the airlock, a half-empty bottle of white rum in one hand, a liter of water in the other. Nkrumah holds a keycard in her hand, and she's waiting next to the interior airlock door, ready to scan it.

"You can't do this," Jacques says for the twentieth time. He shuffles his feet in the several inches of sand that coat the airlock floor. Sweat is already beading on his brow. "Please. I'll die out there. You know I will. Kinsey, you're the team lead. You can stop this. You can make a different decision."

Kinsey feels like the underside of her skin is erupting in hidden hives. Because he's right. She could stop this. But stopping this would mean admitting the reason why she thinks he's not infected. It would mean letting her team—what's left of them—know the most urgent desire of her secret heart. It would mean letting them know how deeply she wants the virus to stay.

So she loads her voice with authority, even as she doesn't meet Jacques's eye. "This *is* my decision. It's just for a few hours," she says. "Just until we figure out what's going on. The storm died down already. You'll be perfectly safe."

That, at least, doesn't feel like a lie. The wind isn't tearing at the walls of the base anymore. The sky is probably clear by now. It'll be as blue as a butterfly wing out there, Kinsey figures. Hopes.

Jacques takes a halting step toward the inner door. "You're not going to figure out what's going on. You're going to kill each other. Please, just—at least lock me in one of the rooms inside, like you did with Domino and Saskia."

Nkrumah shakes her head. "The only other door to shut you behind is a bedroom door. That's too close to where we'll be sleeping. It's not safe."

Jacques looks ready to cry. His eyes jump from face to face, desperately seeking an ally. "Shut me in the airlock, then. You can lock the inner door and I'll stay here. Please," he says again. "It's hot in here, but you know it's hotter out there. And another sandstorm could pick up. Or even just a rainstorm. Anything might happen. I won't make it."

Mads crosses their arms. "What if we have to leave, though? The airlock is the only exit route. We'd be trapped."

Kinsey makes herself look right at Jacques. When he meets her eyes, she feels something, but she can't be sure if it's attraction or exhaustion. She hasn't eaten since— she tries to remember, can't. Her head swims. "I'm sorry," she says. "I really am. But my decision is final. You have to go."

He looks into each of their eyes one last time before giving a slow nod. "Okay," he finally says. "Just for a few hours. Right? Come get me. I'll wait in the shade on the southeast side of the station." His voice breaks. "I don't suppose I can have my keycard, can I?"

Mads looks at their feet, shakes their head. Nkrumah looks at the ceiling, scrubs her cheek with the heel of one hand while scanning his keycard with the other. Kinsey forces herself to keep her eyes on Jacques. She watches as he bows his head, watches as he turns away, watches every step he takes toward the exterior door. Nkrumah follows him, a few paces behind, ready to lock him out.

When the door opens, the light outside is deep red. It's quiet out there. A soft wind blows eddies of sand across the threshold. Not even a sliver of blue sky is visible.

"What is this?" Jacques says softly, stepping out into the red desert. "No. Wait, don't send me out there. The storm isn't—"

Nkrumah shuts the door behind him before he can finish saying what the storm isn't. Kinsey doesn't blink until the keypad beeps twice, promising that the lock has slid home.

The entire time Jacques was on his way out, she was

waiting for a tell—waiting for the creature he is to reveal itself to her. A wink, a glance, a slipped detail. Her attention pools in her own legs, her belly, the back of her neck; she searches for her own arousal like it's a pin dropped on thick carpet.

She doesn't find anything but a closed door.

When the three of them are back inside, Mads locks the exterior door behind them. Nkrumah lets out a shaky sigh. Kinsey turns to the two of them and crosses her arms. "Okay. Time to figure out what we're going to do."

"Oh, that's easy," Nkrumah laughs.

"It is?"

"I think it's obvious what we're going to do, Boss," Nkrumah says, her voice flat with certainty. "We're going to die."

Nkrumah carries a laundry basket down the residential hall. She's barefoot, stepping carefully, moving silently. She walks with her knees bent and her hips low. Her eyes are on the floor.

She almost makes it to the end of the hall when a door clicks open behind her. She winces, closing her eyes.

"Oh, hey, are you doing laundry?" Jacques asks, poking his head out of the bedroom he shares with Saskia.

"I'm doing *my* laundry," Nkrumah replies. "Mine and Domino's. Our room *only*."

"Can I throw something in there? Just one second." He disappears into his room, ignoring Nkrumah's furious groan.

Mads opens their door at the sound of swearing. "What's going on?" they ask, their voice sleep-fuzzed. When they spot the laundry basket in Nkrumah's arms, their eyes light up. "Someone's doing laundry?"

"No. I'm throwing everything in this basket out into the desert. Don't—" She gives up as Mads emerges into the hall, bed linens wadded in their arms.

"Thank you so much," they say warmly, dropping their bed linens on top of hers and Domino's. "So nice of you."

Nkrumah glowers at them. "I hate this game. I did not agree to play this game. It's not funny and it never has been."

But it's too late. Kinsey opens her door and rains underwear down onto the pile of bed linens. Jacques comes back out with a pile of stinking, sweat-soaked shirts. Saskia shoves socks down into the overfull basket.

"Nkrumah, you are just the best," Domino purrs. "We appreciate you so much."

Nkrumah kicks the basket down the hall, toward the canteen, where the tiny washing machine will take all day to work through the several loads of laundry that have been compressed into the basket. "You're all hanging your own sheets up," she calls over her shoulder. "And next time I catch one of you on your way down the hall, you're getting *all* my underwear. Just you wait."

Mads blows her a kiss. "Thanks!"

The three of them sit on the floor. Nkrumah's back is to the residential hall; Mads's back is to the canteen hall. Kinsey's back is to the lab hall.

None of them wants to have their back to the door they just closed on Jacques.

"Let's try to stay realistic," Mads says. "I know this is scary, but there's no reason to think we're all going to die."

Nkrumah slouches, flicking the keycard rhythmically with her thumb. "It's weird to me that you said 'let's stay realistic' and then followed that immediately with something that has absolutely zero grounding in reality. We have every reason to think we're all going to die, Mads. I don't know if you noticed, but three of our colleagues are gone, the weather is fucked, and all of us are losing the ability to cope."

Kinsey swallows. "We might be able to get our people back, though. We might be able to cure them."

Nkrumah closes her eyes. "Why do I have to be the voice of reason? They've been replaced. Replaced means dead. That thing Domino found in the desert," she adds, her eyes snapping open again to fix on Kinsey, "killed them. Do you understand? They're dead. And we're next. Unless we leave, which . . ."

Kinsey meets Nkrumah's unforgiving gaze. "Which we can't. It's still storming out there, even if the wind has been quiet for the last hour or so. It's high in the atmosphere right now, but it'll drop."

"That's why the sky is still red," Mads says with slow-dawning comprehension. "Domino told me about this once. The storm is moving fast enough to lift sand up into the stratosphere."

"But it can't stay there for long," Nkrumah says. "It's incredible that it's stayed that high for so long already."

As if on cue, there's a soft patter on the ceiling. It dies away fast, like a brief scattering of early rain before a storm, but the three of them freeze. Kinsey doesn't doubt that they're all thinking of Jacques.

"It won't all come down here," Mads says. "The winds at that altitude are fast. They'll carry the sand faster than we can imagine. Like those frog eggs in Birmingham, remember? It ended up raining tadpoles in Santa Cruz. Anything that gets lifted up that high in the air travels, it has to. The sand'll come down miles from here. He'll be fine."

"Even when the storm passes, though," Kinsey ventures. She can tell from the look on Nkrumah's face that she's saying what they're both thinking. "Even then." She feels like she's reciting lines. The words are fat wooden beads strung along a fixed wire in her mind, destined to fall one after the other no matter how she pushes them. "If we leave here, we take the virus with us. We can't risk this spreading beyond the station."

Both of them turn to Mads. It's not fair—Mads is the station doctor, yes, but that role doesn't leave them with the responsibility of deciding whether or not the station is under full quarantine. Still, fair or not, Kinsey and Nkrumah both wait on Mads's decision.

"You're right. We can't leave." They nod to Kinsey. "The virus—or maybe the entire lichen, I don't know—jumped from the specimen to Jacques within minutes of making physical contact, and the rest of us were sick within hours. That means interspecies transmission. And the specimen was—it was buried, right, when you all found it?"

"When Domino found it," Nkrumah corrects. Her gaze drops to the floor when she says Domino's name. Maybe she's remembering how she and Domino had been bickering over the specimen as they brought it inside. Maybe she's realizing that the last thing she said to them before they were taken over by the virus was *who digs a hole just to piss?*

"Right. So it was buried, which means it was probably dead, or at least in some kind of deep torpor, before Domino dug it up. That indicates the lichen can potentially live in dead tissue."

"Feed on dead tissue," Kinsey ventures. "I mean—it's a fungus. It can do more than just inhabit a dead thing. It can feed."

"Which means there's no downside to the death of the host," Nkrumah finishes. "The only thing that can prevent spread is isolation. So we agree we can't leave, yes? And we can't call for help when the phone and Wi-Fi come back online, because anyone who comes here will get infected, too."

"Unless we destroy it somehow," Kinsey adds thoughtfully. "What kills viruses? Fire, alcohol . . . ?"

Nkrumah clicks her tongue ring against her teeth thoughtfully. "Antibodies, but we don't have any of those lying around. Not for this one, anyway."

"Well, maybe we do, though," Mads says. "I mean, the three of us all got sick, but didn't get taken over, right? So we might have antibodies."

Nkrumah looks sidelong at Mads, then briefly glances at Kinsey before her gaze drops to the linoleum. "We don't know," she replies slowly, "that none of us got taken over."

No one says anything for a long time. The rattle of the ventilation system, the soft patter of sand against the roof, the gentle human sounds of breath and discomfort—all that, but no words, because there's no answer to the point Nkrumah has made. It's the kind of point that divides people into those who can't stand to say the thing, and those who can't stand to leave it unsaid.

"We should bring Jacques back inside," Kinsey says at last. "There's sand hitting the base. Whether it's driving at us or falling on us doesn't matter. If we don't know for sure that Jacques is—"

"I saw what I saw," Nkrumah says in a low, exhausted voice.

"I believe you," Kinsey says. "What I'm saying is—if we don't know how long the lichen can survive in desert conditions? We don't know how far Jacques can get. He could walk to town. He could walk to Boot Hill."

"What did you ask him?" Mads asks. "Before we decided to make him leave, you asked something. What was it?"

"Yeah, and what's this 'feeling' you seem to have?" Nkrumah adds.

Kinsey considers for a long time before answering. "It's nothing," she says at last.

"I don't think it is," Mads says slowly. "You're the one who first saw that Domino wasn't human anymore. Saskia, too."

Nkrumah sits up a little straighter. "Yeah," she says, eyeing Kinsey. "What tipped you off about them?"

"The extra mouths and eyes and tongues," Kinsey says. "Same as you."

"No other clues?" Mads looks disappointed, almost desperate. "There must be something."

Kinsey shakes her head. "Nothing."

"That's bullshit," Nkrumah says. Kinsey's still not looking at her, but the force of her gaze is laserlike. "There *was* something. You said that Domino was acting weird before the thing with all the mouths."

"Did I? I don't remember saying that." Kinsey's clothes feel too tight all of a sudden. She tugs at the neck of her shirt, trying to loosen it, then sits on her hands when she realizes she's performing a cartoonishly obvious pantomime of *hiding something*.

"You did. You did say it," Mads says, their posture sharpening in a mirror of Nkrumah's. The mood between the two of them has shifted from defeat to attention.

"I remember," Nkrumah says, gaining momentum. "You said something about how they acted when you were showering. Their hair dried too fast, right? And you said—"

"She said that they probably only wanted to look at the specimen in order to get her alone," Mads finishes. "What made you think that? Was it something in their tone, or their affect, or—"

Kinsey wishes the station had a window she could climb out of. Her heart is a trapped grasshopper slamming against the glass jar of her body. She shrugs. "I don't know, I just . . . I probably just thought that in hindsight?"

"Think," Nkrumah urges. "Think back. It could help. Come on, you were in the shower, and . . . ?"

"And, I don't know, they were kind of"—she doesn't want to say it, she has no choice but to say it—"flirting with me?"

Mads shakes their head. "We knew that. They came on to you in the exam room, right? And—"

"What about Saskia?" Nkrumah interrupts. "When I was moving the bookshelves with Jacques, she was calling your name through the lab door. Did she come on to you too?"

Kinsey shrugs. "Maybe?" The lie feels like cooling candle wax on her tongue. "I don't know, I can never tell when someone's flirting with me. Are you sure it was my name she was saying?"

"I heard it too," Mads says. "And she was staring at you a lot when we were talking about splitting up to check each other over. She was doing that thing," they add, lifting a hand to their throat.

"Oh, yeah, the horny necklace thing she does," Nkrumah says, snapping and pointing at Mads. "That's her tell. She always fidgets with that cross when she's turned on."

Kinsey holds her hands up, trying to stop them. "Guys, stop. None of that makes any sense," she says. "Why would the lichen—why would it have the same tells as Saskia? That doesn't—"

"It replicated Domino well enough to whistle," Nkrumah says. She's picking up speed, gaining enthusiasm. "Yesterday I could hear them whistling in the shower from clear down the hall. Obviously the lichen is picking up our behaviors too. Neural pathway mirroring, maybe? Kinsey, think hard, okay, this is important." She studies Kinsey's face with rapt intensity. "Did Saskia flirt with you?"

Kinsey closes her eyes. Remembers the chill of Saskia's necklace pressing into the nape of her neck. She feels briefly dizzy with need. "I think so," she says weakly. "Yeah, I think she might have."

"That's it, then," Nkrumah says, pushing herself to her feet. "The lichen wants Kinsey. Mads, are you horny for Kinsey?"

"Uh," Mads says, "I don't—"

"Because I'm not horny for Kinsey," Nkrumah continues, seemingly oblivious to Mads's discomfort. "So you and I are fine, then. Kinsey, sorry, I'm not gonna ask if you're horny for yourself, you'd just lie anyway if you were."

"I wouldn't—wait," Kinsey says.

But it's too late. Nkrumah has momentum, and she's not stopping for anyone. "This is an easy solve," she says, turning her entire body to face Mads. "We just have to kill Kinsey."

Kinsey is on her feet before she knows she's about to stand. "What? No, that's—"

"We've been thinking about this all wrong. It wants Kinsey. It's only pursuing Kinsey. Think about it, Mads," Nkrumah says eagerly. "Domino didn't try anything with you when you went into that room, right? They didn't try to hurt you, they didn't even try to touch you."

"Definitely didn't flirt with me," Mads says, frowning thoughtfully. "That's true. It doesn't seem compulsive. Honestly, it doesn't even seem malicious. Maybe we're jumping to conclusions here. We've been reacting with fear but we have no proof that this lichen wants to *hurt* us."

That's too much for Kinsey. "It doesn't matter if it doesn't want to hurt us," she says. The sand on the roof is louder now, tapping like Nkrumah's finger on the exam room glass. Kinsey doesn't want to say any of this. Speaking it out loud is almost unbearably painful—it's the thing she never lets herself think, never lets herself look at straight on. "They're viruses. A virus doesn't want to hurt anyone, it just wants to live. It just wants to survive and propagate. It can't help the fact that its very existence hurts everything it touches. It can't help it," she says again, her voice breaking on a sob. "But that's what we can't afford to forget—whether it wants to kill us or not, killing is all it's capable of. We can't forget that. People will die if we do."

Mads regards her. Then their gaze shifts behind her, to stare down the corridor where Domino's and Saskia's doubles lie in wait. "You're both right," they say.

Kinsey doesn't like the resignation in their voice. "How do you mean?"

They're quiet for a long time. They won't look away from the lab corridor. Their shoulders rise, then slump forward. When they finally answer her, they sound hollowed out. "Kinsey, you're right that it doesn't matter what the lichen wants—it's dangerous. And Nkrumah, you're right that we should kill Kinsey."

Kinsey takes a half step backward, away from them both. "What?!"

"Not just you," Mads says, as though that's better. "It's not just you that needs to die. It's all three of us. And Saskia, and Domino. And Jacques, too," they add, glancing toward the door to the airlock. "We should bring him inside and kill him. And then we should burn this place to the ground."

"Mads—"

Mads rubs their eyes, digging their knuckles into the deep hollows of fatigue there. "It's the only way to make sure we eliminate the lichen completely. So none of us can risk transmitting it to the rest of the world."

Kinsey looks back and forth between them. "You can't be serious. We're not killing ourselves. That's—it's just not what we're doing," she says, feeling ridiculous as the first real flutter of panic unfurls inside of her. "No. There has to be a better solution. There's always a better solution."

"Not this time," Nkrumah says. Her eyes are still bright, her expression still engaged and enthusiastic—but her face isn't moving. It's a mask, Kinsey realizes, and it's stuck. "I can go get the field rifle from the Jeep. Let's not waste time. Mads, are any of the cleaning supplies in the storage closet good for accelerant?"

"Wait." Kinsey's entire body is buzzing. "Wait wait wait. Stop. Please—there's something I haven't told you."

Mads and Nkrumah both turn to face her. They look energized, terrified, determined. They look ready to face death—but when Kinsey speaks, they still listen. They wait for her to tell them the thing that will change their minds and save them all.

She has to save them all.

"I—" Kinsey freezes, realizes that everything she hasn't said, every secret she's holding, has the potential to make things worse. It doesn't matter. She has to say something. She has to stop them. "I never got sick," she says at last.

"What do you mean? Of course you did," Mads says, frowning. "We all did."

"I didn't. I lied. I just didn't want to catch what everyone else had. I stayed in my room for a few days while the rest of you got sick, but I was fine the whole time."

"But you were one of the first ones who got sick," Nkrumah says, tilting her head to one side. "You couldn't have known that everyone would—"

"Mads called quarantine," Kinsey interrupts. "I figured, better safe than sorry. I shouldn't have lied," she adds, hoping that admitting this small failure will save her from having to own up to any bigger ones. "It was selfish of me. I just didn't know how to tell you before now. I'm sorry."

"It doesn't matter," Mads says.

"Of course it does." Kinsey needs it to. "I don't—I don't want to die. And since I didn't get sick, we know the virus didn't get me. Maybe I'm immune or something," she says, trying desperately to iron the tremble out of her voice. "I can go get help. I can go tell someone what's happening. I can—"

"It doesn't matter," Mads says again, more firmly this time. "Just because you didn't have symptoms, that doesn't mean you didn't get the virus. You could be a carrier. Hell, for all we know, you could be an incubator."

"I'm not—"

"It's not a chance we can afford to take," Mads says. "If this lichen gets out of the desert, that's an extinction-level event. This thing kills whatever it touches and eats whatever it kills. It would wipe out humanity."

"It would wipe out everything," Nkrumah breathes. Her adrenaline seems to be ebbing at last. Her shoulders slump, her chin sinking to her chest. "Everything. Gone. We have to. We have to—shit. God damn it. Fuck."

Kinsey reaches a tentative hand toward Nkrumah, rests it on her shoulder. "This is too big for us to figure out right now," Kinsey says. She tries to make it gentle, soft. She tries not to sound terrified. "We're all exhausted and scared and overwhelmed. Let's sleep on it, okay?"

"What's the point?" Nkrumah asks. "Sleeping won't make the situation any better."

SPREAD ME

"No," Kinsey agrees, "but it might make us smarter. There are answers. We just have to come up with them."

Mads nods. "Okay."

"Really?" Kinsey's head swims with relief.

"Yeah, fine," Nkrumah agrees. "Eight hours. We meet back here—"

"In the canteen," Kinsey interrupts. "I want to sit on a couch."

"Fine," Nkrumah says. She sounds more exhausted by the second. "We all need to eat something. I gotta put this fucking thing back on the pile," she adds, brandishing the keycard she used to exile Jacques. "But if nobody has a better idea eight hours from now, we end this. Deal?"

Kinsey gives her shoulder a soft squeeze. "Deal."

They walk down the hall to their respective bedrooms in silence. Kinsey locks her door, then leans against it, staring at the painting on her wall and hoping an answer will come to her before dawn.

Jacques is scrubbing the lab tables. Soapy water, a soft yellow sponge, his arms rhythmically pumping across the stainless steel. His shirt hangs out of the back pocket of his cutoffs. It sways in time with the rocking of his shoulders and hips.

Mads stands in the doorway to the lab, their arms folded across their chest. They came to ask Kinsey for something—she's at a microscope, recording the diameters of cryptobiotic fungal hyphae from the previous day's samples. Mads loves coming to request equipment and supplies while she's recording data, because they know she hates the distraction and will say yes just to make them go away.

But they're not asking her for anything yet. They're just standing there, watching Jacques work. Their expression is placid, but their head is tilted at a curious angle. "You do this every morning," they observe.

"Mm," Jacques responds, not looking around at them.

"Nobody even used the lab yesterday. You were all in the field all day long. That table is still clean from the last time you scrubbed it."

Jacques dunks the sponge into the plastic bin of suds, wrings it out. "That's true."

"What do you need, Mads?" Kinsey asks, adjusting the focus on the scope even though she can already see perfectly clearly. This is why she doesn't like distractions. They make her fidget.

"I need to know why Jacques is cleaning a clean surface. Could be a sign of desert madness."

Jacques pauses in his scrubbing. "There's no such thing as 'desert madness.'"

Mads clicks their tongue. "That's one of the hallmark symptoms of desert madness. Denial."

Kinsey turns around on the lab stool. She twitches her pencil between her fingers, drumming it against her thigh. "Jacques, this isn't fair to you, but I need to ask you to please tell Mads why you scrub the lab every morning. Otherwise, they are going to keep being annoying until I succumb to desert madness and stab them through the eyeball with this pencil."

"Aw, Boss. You could never have desert madness." Mads's face is alight with mischief. "I've never *once* seen you scrub a lab table."

Jacques wipes down the surface of the table with the sponge, letting the dead suds splatter against the linoleum floor. He'll come back through with a mop once he's finished with the surfaces, just like he does every morning. "I like a clean lab," he says, shrugging his freckle-blotted shoulders and moving to the next lab table. "A clean lab produces clean results."

"Last night," Mads says, "I watched you drink gin and canned pineapple syrup off the small of Nkrumah's back. Since when are you dedicated to cleanliness? Of any kind?"

Kinsey stops drumming her pencil, looking between the two of them. "Wait, you two are—"

"No," Jacques says, "but Nkrumah left the door open and someone poked their head in to ask about tetanus shots."

"Gin and canned pineapple syrup sounds good," Kinsey mutters.

"It was. And Mads—I clean the lab every morning because it's the right thing to do. Okay?" Jacques's voice is easy, but there's a warning on the horizon of it. "I'm not a complete disaster, no matter what people think."

Kinsey's and Mads's eyes meet briefly. Mads raises their eyebrows. "Got it. Sorry for interrupting. Kinsey, you got a minute to talk about gloves? We need a non-latex brand, Saskia's developing a sensitivity."

Kinsey rises. "Tell me about it in the exam room. I need to get away from these samples for a minute anyway."

As they leave, Jacques starts humming to himself. It's a song Domino has been whistling lately, and it's in all their heads. They can hear the tune all the way down the hall.

Kinsey manages to keep it together for four hours, as the sand falls and the wind picks back up. Soon, it's howling again, harder than ever, scouring the outside of the little wedge they all live in. She listens to the world screaming over the vast expanse of desert that surrounds the base, and she tries her damnedest to think of a solution to the problem of the lichen.

It's the most important thing she'll ever do, she knows. Solving this matters more than anything. It matters more than the thought of Jacques, trapped outside in all that Hell. It matters more than the fact that Domino and Saskia are just a few walls away, locked in the exam room and the lab, waiting for her.

Wanting her.

But her body doesn't seem to share her priorities. Her

skin is too sensitive, her legs restless. She can't get comfortable in her bed. She leans against the warm wall, feeling it cool as the temperature plummets outside. She catches herself trailing fingers across her limbs, following the path Saskia forged. She strokes the tender skin of her own underarm, then the crease where her hip blends into her thigh.

They feel the same. Maybe, she thinks, they are the same. Maybe it's not so complicated to transform one into the other, to open oneself up and become a sweet slick of invitation.

She's going to go to the exam room, she decides. She's going to pull the cardboard off the window and press her nose to the glass and tell Domino that she's sorry. That they were right, and she overreacted. That she shouldn't have told everyone to look at their mistake. It was a small mistake, she thinks, and it didn't deserve that kind of attention. A few extra eyes, a few extra mouths—so what? What does it matter? In the face of such perfect, total becoming, who cares if a few pieces get mixed up?

At the same moment that she opens her door, Mads opens theirs, too. Kinsey freezes, thwarted. They stare at each other across the hall. Then Mads, glancing at Nkrumah's door, steps out of their bedroom and into the hallway.

"What are you doing?" they whisper.

"Going to the bathroom," Kinsey lies. "What are you doing?"

"Same. Do you want to go first?"

Kinsey nods, biting back a swear. She pads down the hall to the bathroom. Avoids making eye contact with the double shower. As she sits on the toilet, she considers what she'd been about to do. The second she was snapped out of her own libidinous reverie, she could see how unhinged her plan had been. If she'd gone to the exam room as she'd intended, would she be able to resist going inside? If she'd gone inside, would she have been able to keep Domino contained? If she hadn't—where might they have gone? What might they have done?

Kinsey decides that she can't be trusted. She's not strong enough in the face of this kind of temptation. When she comes back from the bathroom, she catches Mads by the arm. "I haven't been drinking nearly enough water," she whispers. "When I tried to piss, my urethra coughed. Hydrate with me when you get back?"

"Sure." Mads looks at her with eyes that are too understanding. They think she's afraid to be alone. She doesn't correct them.

She waits in their room. They've got both twin beds pushed together against one wall, a thick stack of blankets piled into a nest to try to make up for the crack between the small mattresses. There are photos taped to the walls. Kinsey looks them over in the dim light of the single scarf-draped lamp.

There's an older couple, one of whom has Mads's hawklike nose. A woman, mid-laugh, holding up what looks like a plate of shrimp. A house with a jasmine-choked trellis in front. She's still looking the photos over when the door opens behind her and Mads slips inside, carrying two enormous bottles of water.

"Is this your girlfriend?" Kinsey asks, gesturing to the woman with the shrimp.

"Sister," Mads says, handing her a bottle of water.

"What's with the shrimp?"

"It's an inside joke."

"I don't want to die," Kinsey blurts. Heat floods her face. "Sorry. I don't—I didn't mean—"

"It's okay," Mads says. They sink to the floor, leaning back against the bed. "Nobody wants to die."

Kinsey sits on the floor opposite them, her back to the wall. "Some people do."

"Nah. Not really."

"I think yes-really. They have hotlines about it."

Mads crumples half their face, twists their shoulders in a pantomime of complication. "People who want to die don't actually want to be dead," they say slowly, feeling their way through the thought as they put voice to it. "They just want something to be different, something that feels like it can't change any other way. So the only real way they can figure out how to change their circumstances is by dying. And sometimes they're right. Sometimes, there's really no better option. But mostly it's just that the other options feel more impossible than they really are. Wanting something impossibly different—that feels like wanting to die, sure. But it's not the same as wanting to be dead."

Kinsey swallows a too-large gulp of water, coughs. "Shit," she says after she's sure she can breathe, "you've thought about this a lot."

"Yeah. I think about it a lot. Used to think about it a lot more." They shoot Kinsey a sidelong glance. "The point is, nobody wants to die, but that doesn't mean nobody *has* to die."

"Maybe you have a point, though. About other options feeling more impossible than they really are."

Mads doesn't answer right away. They drink their water, their eyes on the floor. "I think," they say slowly, "it's different for us. We aren't talking about dying because we can't stand the way our lives feel right now. We already know that we don't want to die. But we have to. It's our responsibility to die."

"Is that how Nkrumah sees things?"

"I think so. I don't think she's happy about this outcome. She's just . . . certain."

Kinsey smiles down at the water bottle in her lap. "That's Nkrumah. She always knows exactly what she thinks."

They sit in silence for a few minutes, drinking water, listening to the wind. It almost seems to have a voice. Kinsey wonders if Domino is screaming in the exam room, if Saskia has started yelling for freedom again. If Jacques is still able to scream, out there in the storm. She wonders if she'd be able to hear him, if he was.

Mads interrupts her thoughts. "Do you ever wish you had that? The certainty Nkrumah has?"

"I think I do," Kinsey says. "I just don't always want to admit what I think. But that's not the same thing as not knowing."

Mads regards her. "Yeah. I think I know what you mean. I think I see that in you. You've got stuff buried."

"Only a couple of feet down, though."

A look comes over Mads, a deep consideration. "Why don't you want to tell us about that stuff? The stuff you have buried?"

Kinsey thinks it over. "How much do you know about the thing we're studying out here? The cryptobiotic crust?"

"Less than I should," Mads answers right away. "I mean, I don't study it. I just came here to make sure none of you die from diarrhea or whatever. So I know about, like, dehydration and scorpions. And Jacques told me something about algae a while ago. But I probably don't know about whatever you're thinking of right now. Tell me?"

Kinsey can't help but grin. This is a part of Mads she adores—the endless curiosity, the genuine interest in other people. Mads always wants to know more, always wants to learn, never gets defensive about the things they don't know or don't understand.

She can't imagine them dying. She can't imagine that part of them disappearing forever.

The pain of that thought is ignorable, though, so she ignores it and leans forward, still grinning. She launches into her pitch, the pitch she made to each team member she hired herself. It feels obscenely good to return to something so familiar. "Okay, so. The thing about the desert is, it's alive. It's—why are you looking at me like that?" she asks, noticing the horrified expression on their face.

Mads shakes their head, takes a few short, quick breaths. "Nothing. I just—I remembered the part Jacques told me, about all the algaes and stuff below the soil. Tell me the rest."

Kinsey hesitates, wanting to press—but Mads gestures impatiently for her to continue, so she does. She continues clumsily, her momentum lost. "Anyway, um. Yeah. It's all algaes and lichens and stuff below the surface, like Jacques told you. And . . . it's like that with me. If you dig up the cryptobiotic crust, it dies. And when it dies, the whole ecosystem dies. That's part of how we got the dust bowl, you know? It was the destruction of grassland root systems, but it was also the constant tilling. The soil couldn't form a fungal network to keep the surface soil in place, so the wind just . . ." She makes a vague sweeping gesture with her hands. "And that's how I feel sometimes. Like if I dig all the stuff up to show people, then the stuff will die, and I'll die too."

Mads takes a long slug from their water bottle, wipes their mouth on the back of their wrist. "Well. You're gonna die anyway. You might as well tell me your big secret."

Kinsey manages an anemic laugh. "Hey, look. I can tell

I said something that hit you wrong. If we're going to die, I don't want my last thought to be, *what did I do to upset Mads*. Will you tell me what happened there?"

Mads looks all around the room. Everywhere that isn't Kinsey. They stand up and look at the pictures on the wall, look at the door, smooth the covers on the bed. Finally, when Kinsey can't stand it anymore, they clear their throat. "The cryptobiotic crust," they say. "I've heard you guys talking about it, and I haven't paid much attention because, to be honest, I just—I don't know, it seems too complicated. But the thing is—fuck." They press their head against the wall, their voice thick. "Fuck."

"Woah. Hey, what's going on?" Kinsey stands and takes a step closer to them, not sure whether or not she should reach out or leave them alone. "Mads?"

"The crust. The cryptobiotic crust. It's a living thing, right?"

"Well—no? It's not just one creature, it's a whole network. It's a living thing the way a coral reef is a living thing."

"Right. Okay. But that means it's all connected. Which means that this lichen we discovered—it can live down there." They straighten. Their forehead is red where it was pressed against the wall. Tears stream freely down their cheeks. "It might have been living down there all along. It could be propagating all across the desert. The virus probably spread to whatever else is living down there, way before you guys dug up that specimen. Who knows how long it's been down there. Who knows how far it's already spread."

Kinsey feels everything in her body go still. "That can't be right," she whispers, even as she knows that it is. "The lichen we're dealing with is like nothing we've ever seen before. It's got to be specific to one kind of fungus, right?

It's not like a virus that size can be supported by just any network of hyphae."

"That's a good point," Mads says, letting their head fall back on a mirthless laugh. Their tears stream across their temples, soaking into their hair. "You know viruses. Notoriously unadaptable. Wouldn't *dream* of mutating to gain access to a more favorable environment."

Kinsey feels a faint thrill of hope. Even if Mads and Nkrumah get to see their plan through—even if the three of them die and the station ends up a smoking pile of ashes—that won't be the end of the virus. It's a feeling she knows she shouldn't have, but she can't help having it.

This is why she put herself into exile in the first place. She can't help rooting for the wrong team.

Kinsey drains the last of her water, then screws the cap onto the empty bottle and tosses it at Mads. It hits them in the arm, and they look up, startled. "Fine," Kinsey says. "Everyone's going to die and we're all doomed, so we might as well get drunk. It'll be easier to kill ourselves if we're hungover. Won't feel like much of a loss, right? Do you still have your secret stash?"

Mads looks at her blankly, then bursts out laughing. It's the kind of laughter that comes out like vomit, a cleansing hysteria that turns into silent gasping before it eases off. "I didn't know you knew about that," they say at last.

"Everyone knows about it," she says, then winces internally at the way "everyone" has diminished. "It's the only booze here that we can be sure Jacques won't drink."

Mads dives to the floor, reaches under their bed, and fishes around for a moment before emerging with a mostly full bottle of whiskey. They open Kinsey's empty water bottle and pour in a few glugs, then take a pull directly from the whiskey bottle. The two of them sit on the bed and toast each other.

"To the end of everything we ever loved," Kinsey says.

Mads meets her water bottle with their whiskey bottle. "To the end."

Saskia sits on the floor of Kinsey's bedroom, her legs crossed. She's rolling joints for Jacques, who is giving up alcohol for a week to prove a point to Mads. Saskia doesn't smoke, but she has deft hands and loves repetitive tasks, so there are twenty neat, compact joints in a row on the floor in front of her.

"Vareniki and pelmeni are different," she's explaining. Kinsey is only half listening, but that doesn't deter Saskia. "With vareniki you cook the filling ahead of time. Pelmeni, you fill raw. It's a completely different vibe."

"Right." Kinsey adds another line to the email she's drafting to TQI, asking for an increased grocery budget. She deletes the line, then puts it back in. "And pelmeni is the sweet one?"

"Never," Saskia says vehemently. "You don't listen, Kinsey.

That one is never sweet." She runs her tongue along the edge of a rolling paper. "I'll make them for you and you'll understand. Can we get ground pork? Will TQI let us have that?"

Kinsey considers. "I think so? But you should talk to Nkrumah, I think she doesn't do pork."

"Beef," Saskia says. "She had a pet cow when she was young. But either way, I could do a mushroom filling. What you don't understand is that it's really all about the wrapper. You have to roll it so thin . . ."

She keeps going. Her words wash over Kinsey like puffs of smoke. She describes stewing sweet spiced cherries, mixing sour cream with horseradish, chopping dunes of dill and toasting walnuts. She rolls joints until she's gone through Domino's entire stash of rolling papers. The floral sap-smell of decent weed fills the room.

It takes Kinsey an hour to write the email to TQI. She asks for special budgetary allowances for cherries and ground pork. Saskia is there the entire time. It's only the next morning that Kinsey stops to consider that Saskia was keeping her company, so she didn't have to work alone.

Kinsey wakes up gently. She doesn't open her eyes, doesn't move her body. She's warm. It's quiet. Her skull hisses with the static noise of a not-quite-hangover, the impact of whiskey and panic gentled by an enormous amount of water and the gravity of deep sleep. She can feel the worse that might have been, but miraculously, there's no headache waiting to reveal itself—there's only the soft velvet cushion of deep exhaustion, waiting for her to sink into it.

As she pushes her face into her pillow, Kinsey is struck by the kind of wisdom that lives on the cusp of unconsciousness, the kind of thought that she won't be able to grasp when she's fully awake. Exhaustion, she realizes, is only unpleasant when one has to resist it. But when succumbing is an option—when everything is still and quiet and there's no reason to push the strong arms of sleep away—exhaustion is ecstasy.

A solid band of pressure at her midsection stops her from rolling onto her stomach. She lets her hands drift toward her stomach, fingers spider-walking over the blankets to try to find whatever tangle in them has got her stuck in place. But where she'd expect to find a thick twist of fabric, her hands instead encounter warm, well-muscled flesh.

Her eyes snap open. On a deep breath, Kinsey arches her back. Her spine curls, her ribs expand, and she feels herself pressing into the soft wall of a chest. *Mads*, she thinks, connecting the sensation with the smell of someone else's sweat on the pillow, fuzzy memories of the night before. She's in Mads's bed. She's in Mads's arms.

Their belly fits perfectly into the small of her back. As the tide of sleep pulls away from her brain, it leaves recognizable sensations behind: warm breath on the back of her neck, pressure on the back of her head where Mads's forehead must be pressed into her hair. They're wrapped around her like a tongue cupping a sip of soup.

It's nice.

Enjoying this moment is a new experience for Kinsey. She doesn't want to surge away from Mads, like she normally would. Their skin against hers isn't a clammy smothering hell. It reminds her of the first time she enjoyed wine, when the sour burn she'd always hated transmuted itself into something warm and complex and really very pleasant.

Kinsey is wearing only her shirt and underwear, a state of undress that she's starting to associate with Mads. Mads, as far as she can tell, is in their underwear and nothing else. She doesn't remember falling asleep here, but she does have a vague recollection of pulling her bra off through one shirtsleeve, announcing herself the champion of locker-room modesty.

It's pleasant, being half-undressed next to Mads. Maybe there will be embarrassment later. That doesn't matter. "Later" is a distant shoreline.

She swims her bare legs through the blankets, searching for theirs, wanting to feel the closeness of them along the entire length of her body. She only finds a thin layer of grit between the sheets. They shift in their sleep, tighten their grip around her. She hears a soft murmur from just behind one of her ears, goes still to try to keep from waking them. Once they seem settled, she sends her legs searching again.

This time, she does find something. Her foot meets something solid, something that's tangled up in the blankets. She nudges her way past fabric, searching Mads out, her mind already sinking back into sleep. Her ankle slides between two strong, heavy legs, her foot sliding along the arch of Mads's foot, her knee notching in over theirs.

Mads shifts behind her, nuzzles their face into the back of her hair. They make a strange, wet snuffling sound. It's enough to fully banish the promise of sleep, and with no small amount of regret, she accepts that she's awake. Whatever that sound was, it's more important than the deep black bliss of unconsciousness.

"You okay?" she whispers.

They don't reply.

"Hey," she says softly, lacing her fingers through theirs and squeezing their hand where it rests over her belly. Memories of the day before are coming into full focus in her mind. Mads had stopped crying when they'd started drinking. Maybe sobriety is bringing the tears back to them. "It's okay. We'll figure something out. Nkrumah's probably not even awake yet, we'd have heard her thumping around. We've got time. Yeah?"

They still don't say anything. Their arms are tight around her, and they sniff into the back of her hair again. They sound deeply congested. She wonders briefly how long they were crying before she woke up, how she didn't notice sooner.

"Mads? Here, let me—" She pulls away. Mads clings to her, tries to prevent her from turning over in the bed, but she extracts herself from their arms. "I don't even remember falling asleep," she says as she stretches to reach for the bedside lamp. "When did we turn the lights off?"

There's no answer. Kinsey turns the lamp on, blinks briefly in the light. Then she turns over to look Mads in the eyes.

But there are no eyes to meet.

It takes Kinsey a second to understand what she's seeing: curled up between her and the wall, half-tangled in the blankets, is the specimen from the desert. Its head rests on Mads's pillow, a soft spill of sand from one of the eye sockets scattered across the sheets. Its neck vanishes into a dune of bedding.

But Kinsey knows what she felt—fingers, toes, the silk of bare skin against hers. None of that belonged to the specimen. None of that was wrapped around her.

She whips the bedsheets back and sees the rest.

It's Mads. Mads's arms, Mads's legs, Mads's belly. It's their body—unmistakable, underwear-clad, soft with sleep. But it stops at the shoulders, becoming something else. The scattered hair that normally peppers Mads's chest is thick now, thick and thicker as it goes up toward a furred neck. The rest of them is gone, replaced by the head of the thing they found in the desert. No soft jaw, no warm eyes, no thick curls.

That, Kinsey understands, is the snuffling she heard: it was the blunt wet coyote-nose of the specimen, breathing into her hair.

Mads is gone. It has devoured them. It has destroyed them. It has replaced them.

Kinsey stumbles backward. The creature in the bed lunges after her. It rises to Mads's knees, reaches toward her with Mads's hand, clutches at her shoulder with Mads's fingers. It draws a rattling breath, sucking air down what sounds like half a windpipe. The breath catches on a chain of dry coughs—the creature doubles over and sand drops out of its open mouth like a broken hourglass, *pat-patting* onto the bedsheets with every lung-cracking heave.

Kinsey doesn't wait to see if the creature will catch its breath. She slips off the edge of the bed. She lands on the pile of discarded clothes and scrambles crabwise for the door.

The creature dives after her. It stretches one of Mads's long muscular arms toward her. Kinsey jerks her legs back but she isn't fast enough—fingers wrap around her ankle, stronger than Mads's grip ever could have been. It jerks her back toward the bed. Her ass slides along the floor, the carpet shearing a layer of skin off the backs of her bare thighs. For a gut-clenching instant she feels the joint creak loose of the socket as the creature hauls her by the ankle.

Pain and fear yank a scream out of her—and to her shock, at the sound of her screaming, the creature lets go.

"Wait," the specimen says. It speaks with a rasping, cracked version of Mads's voice. "Don't run, Kinsey, please just let me explain!"

"Explain what?!" Kinsey yells. "Don't come near me! What did you do to Mads?"

"Mads is gone," the specimen explains. It blinks at

her—one eye socket still full of packed sand, the other half-hollow, revealing a flash of white bone. "But look, it's okay! I talked with Domino and Saskia—"

"What?" For a moment—just an instant—she hopes wildly that maybe the real Domino and Saskia are still alive somewhere, cocooned in silk or buried in tunnels or sealed into the walls, somewhere she can track them down, somewhere she can save them—

"Isn't that what you called those versions of me? Domino, the me with the . . ." It gestures to its armpit. "And Saskia, the one I did a little better with. Isn't that what you named those versions?"

Kinsey shakes her head, covers her mouth with both hands. "No," she moans. "No, no, no, what do you mean you talked to them, what—"

"They told me how things went when they tried to, you know. Connect with you," the specimen says. The euphemism is somehow a thousand times worse than if it had just said *when they tried to fuck you*. "And we figured out what you really want. It's this, right?" It pulls itself to its knees and turns on all fours to face her. It cocks one ear on the coyote-head, sits back on its knees like a dog settling onto its haunches. "It's everything you want. A beautiful body, just like the one on Mads. And the mystery and interest of a novel specimen, just like the body you dug up in the desert. None of the responsibility and sentiment of a human mind," it adds proudly, running a hand over its own sleek head. "But all the landscape of a human body." Its hand drops, skims over Mads's barrel chest and full belly. It dips the hand under the waistband of its boxer briefs.

"Stop," Kinsey breathes. She looks away—but then, unable to help herself, she glances back. Under the thin fabric, Mads's hand is working rhythmically at their crotch. "Stop!"

The hand stills. The coyote-mouth drops open, revealing small, pointed teeth. "What's wrong?" Mads's voice says from somewhere behind those teeth. It's a near-perfect imitation now, all the rough edges nearly gone.

"You have to stop this. All of this," Kinsey says. Her eyes fill with desperate tears. "You can't keep killing my colleagues—my *friends*. Please. You can't keep killing them. I'm—I'm begging you."

The specimen takes a moment to answer. "Okay," it says at last. "But . . . do you have any friends left?"

"Nkrumah. And Jacques," she says without hesitation. "It's not too late for them, is it?"

It doesn't answer.

"Is it?!"

The specimen's head tilts to one side, considering. Then, after a moment, its hand starts to slowly shift between its legs again. "Hard to say," it says in a low purr. "How bad do you want to know?"

Kinsey looks away, swallows hard around the painful lump in her throat. The part of her that wants the virus is drowned beneath the horror of watching this creature violate what it's made of her friend's body. The nausea that rises in her is an immense relief. Finally, *finally*, she can feel something as simple as disgust.

"This isn't a game," she says weakly. The thing that looks like Mads is panting now, breathless. "I'm not bargaining with you. Just tell me if they're still alive. Please."

The creature lets out a groan. Kinsey doesn't wait to see if it's a groan of frustration or of satisfaction. She forces herself to her feet and stumbles on half-numb legs through the door, yelling Nkrumah's name.

She prays there's anyone left at the station who can hear her.

Domino is unpacking. They're nearly done. They pull a shirt and a pair of scissors out of the bottom of their duffel. The shirt is pink. They slip it on and start cutting it across the belly to make it a crop top.

"What does that say?" Kinsey asks from her seat on the second bed in their room. "Is that a baseball team or—" She stops short as she makes sense of the cursive letters across the chest.

"It says *Baby Slut*," Domino replies, their voice slightly muffled as they bow their neck to get a better view of the scissors.

A laugh startles out of Kinsey without her permission. "What the fuck?" she breathes. "Why?!"

"It's a joke from, um." They snip off a loose curl of cotton. "From online. About Kurt Russell in *The*—"

Jacques appears in the door to Domino's room. "Careful," he warns. "She'll make you put cash in the jar."

Domino looks up. "Sorry, I don't think we've met. I'm Domino. What's the jar?"

"Jacques. The jar is Kinsey's cruel punishment to prevent us from having fun while we're here. Nice shirt," he adds, looking Domino up and down.

"I don't see what this shirt has to do with the jar," Kinsey insists. "But either way, it's definitely not lab *or* field appropriate. Have fun wearing it in your room and the canteen, I guess."

Domino finishes cutting off the bottom half of the shirt and grins up at her. "Sure thing, Boss. Whatever you say."

Kinsey slams the door to Mads's room behind her. The hallway is half-dark. In the bathroom at the far end of the hall, the always-on fluorescents buzz. The walls creak under the onslaught of the still-raging sandstorm. She runs, her bare feet skidding on the linoleum as she hurls herself toward Nkrumah's room. She slips on a drift of sand, nearly falls, catches herself. Doesn't look back.

"Nkrumah!" She slaps her palms against the thin particleboard of Nkrumah's door. "Nkrumah, wake up!"

"I'm awake," Nkrumah calls from inside.

Kinsey looks over her shoulder, sees the shadow of the Mads-specimen-creature at the other end of the hall. It's on all fours, silhouetted by the light from the bathroom. She can't see its face but she knows it's looking at her. She always knows when it's looking at her.

"Let me in," she yells. "Let me in right now!"

The reply from inside is a purr. "It's not locked."

Kinsey freezes with her hand halfway to the knob. There was no impatience in Nkrumah's voice, no snap, no bite. Something's wrong.

"Kinsey?" Nkrumah calls again from inside the room. "Are you coming in?"

Kinsey takes a step backward. A lamp-click from inside the bedroom, a spill of buttery light through the crack under the closed door. She glances down the hall, catches the shape of the creature out of the corner of her eye—it hasn't moved, hasn't chased her. She's going to run, she's already decided. Nkrumah is a lost cause, but Jacques— maybe Jacques is still safe. She's going to sprint for the Jeep and scoop up Jacques on her way, and the two of them will get as far from the station as possible before sounding the alarm. Maybe the two of them can make it out of this.

But then she hears a second voice from inside the room. It sounds like Jacques. "Is that Kinsey?"

"It sure is," Nkrumah calls from the other side of the door.

"Kinsey?!" His voice is raw and ragged. Kinsey's body answers before her mind can form a thought. She crashes toward the door, her body slamming into it even as the knob turns under her hand, her momentum carrying her into the room with so much force that she falls headlong into Nkrumah's arms.

"Woah there!" Nkrumah laughs, a light sweet giggle that makes Kinsey's stomach drop. Nkrumah, the real Nkrumah, has never laughed like that in her life. "You okay? You look—"

"No," Kinsey says, clawing her way up Nkrumah's thin

nightshirt to stand upright. "No, don't talk to me, don't say anything. I don't want to hear it. Jacques? Are you in here?"

Nkrumah shifts so her body takes up Kinsey's entire field of vision. "He's fine, don't worry about him. Do you want to shut the door?"

"No," Kinsey says, trying hard to shove Nkrumah out of the way. It doesn't work. She seems rooted to the floor, a boulder dropped in the middle of this bedroom by a glacier a million years ago. She is part of this place. She will not move.

Nkrumah catches Kinsey's hands, folds them between her own. "It's okay. You don't have to do anything," she says, smiling, bending her head low to look into Kinsey's eyes. "I promise."

Kinsey shakes her head, uncomprehending. "What? What does that mean?"

"I get it now," Nkrumah says. Sand brims in her eyes, spills down over her cheeks. "I'm sorry I had it so wrong before."

"I'm sorry I scared you," Mads's voice echoes from the hallway.

Kinsey whips around. The creature is behind her now. It's still in the hall, not crossing the threshold, but it's too close, and she knows she's trapped.

"I won't make that mistake again," Nkrumah whispers, sand gathering at the corners of her mouth. "Just stay right there. You don't have to do anything," she repeats.

"Where's Jacques?" Kinsey's voice comes out low and shaky. "I heard him in here."

"It's okay. He's fine. Me and Domino brought him inside and cleaned him up hours ago." Nkrumah turns—no, rotates, the top half of her body turning out of rhythm with the bottom half, her legs only belatedly unlocking themselves from the floor. "You just stay there. We came up with a plan you're going to love."

Nkrumah glides away and finally, with her out of the way, Kinsey can see Jacques.

Nkrumah's twin bed has been dragged to the center of the room. It's been stripped, the bedding dumped onto the floor in an unceremonious puddle. Jacques lies in the center of the bed.

He is unmistakably dead. His limbs are limp—ankles crossed, wrists tucked up to his chest. His body is curled into a loosely fetal parenthesis, his head tilted backward at an unsurvivable angle.

As Kinsey watches, frozen, Nkrumah climbs onto the bed and pushes at Jacques's shoulder until he flops onto his back.

"Don't—" she starts.

"Hush." A heavy hand falls onto her shoulder—the creature is in the room now, right behind her, too close to ignore. "We understand now. We understand everything."

"It's not that you don't want me," Nkrumah says, pulling her nightshirt off in one fluid movement. She looks over her shoulder, the corners of her grin curling up like burning paper. The virus has replicated her perfectly. Every detail is accurate, right down to the stretch marks that pearlesce across her hips and breasts.

"It's just that you prefer to watch," the creature says with Mads's voice. "That's okay. It's better than okay."

Kinsey shakes her head. "No," she says, "that's not what—"

"It's okay," Jacques says. His head rolls from one side to the other, the movement of his neck loose and uncontrolled. "Kinsey, you don't have to keep pretending you don't want me. Nobody's here except us. And I promise," he adds, tipping his head at a further angle so Kinsey can't avoid seeing the white film over his eyes. "We all want this to happen just as much as you do."

"Everyone wants the same things you want," Nkrumah says, a new rasp in her voice. She spits a dark clot of wet sand into one palm. Reaches down to grip Jacques. Kinsey catches a glimpse of the thick, rigid line of his cock before it's swallowed by Nkrumah's fist. "See?" His hips lift to meet her. She works the length of him with quick, fluid tugs. Kinsey can hear the shifting scrape of wet sand on taut flesh.

"See?" Jacques repeats, thrusting up into Nkrumah's hand, matching her rhythm perfectly.

"See?" the creature asks, pressing Mads's body against Kinsey's back, nudging her ear with the damp sponge of its nose.

"This isn't what I want," Kinsey whispers.

But the truth is that she doesn't know what she wants. She can feel her body responding to the virus. She can feel herself softening and spreading and yearning for it, for the way it's taken everyone as its own, for the invasion and transformation and manipulation.

But the body she can feel—the tight sweet tension at her nipples, the slow heat between her legs, the gooseflesh across the back of her neck—is a million miles away. Because Jacques is dead, and Nkrumah is dead, and Mads is dead, and everyone is dead, and she can't want them and grieve them at the same time. She's full of white static, she's full of molten metal, it's all too much.

Nkrumah doesn't look at Kinsey, doesn't take her attention off Jacques. "Of course this is what you want," she says, rising to her knees to square her hips up with Jacques's. She pauses, positions the tip of his cock between her thighs. "You're soaking. Touch yourself. You'll feel it. You'll understand why I want to feel it. The way you make your own moisture is incredible. We could grow so much together." She eases herself down onto Jacques's length with mechanical precision. "Did you know that this one was a little in love with you? I'm not doing anything with her body that she didn't fantasize about showing you anyway." Beneath her, Jacques rasps out a rough moan and grips her pumping hips with his limp hands. "It's okay to enjoy it."

"Feel," the creature behind Kinsey whispers. It licks the side of her neck with a sandpaper tongue, takes her wrist and pushes her fingers down into the soft damp heat at the center of her. "Don't you feel?"

The touch electrifies her. She still feels far from her body, still can't make sense of the hunger that's been building inside of her—but she can feel that touch on her wrist.

It summons a sudden flash flood of adrenaline that sparks movement into her limbs. She jerks away from the creature, whips around to face it. Surprise freezes it, its eyeless face looking at her without understanding. Kinsey jukes left before lunging to the right, slipping past it. The creature tries to block her. She's too fast. She dodges around it before it can catch her.

"Kinsey, wait," Jacques and Nkrumah call in unison. Mads's fingers snag in her shirt. She hears the fabric tear as she plunges into the darkness of the hallway. She doesn't stop, doesn't slow down. She can't. If she does, she knows she'll turn back.

She needs to be gone before she can change her mind.

"It's not too late to change your mind." The TQI hiring manager, Kathryn Bell, is holding a stack of keycards. Desert dust has already coated her suede ankle boots, and a smear of something white runs up the side of her black trousers like a tuxedo stripe. Her mask is top-of-the-line—fitted cloth with an internal filtration layer, the best possible protection against the new H7N3 strain. "If you don't want to be a desert hermit for the next four years, now's your chance to run."

Kinsey smiles and takes the stack of keycards. She took her own mask off the second she got into the TQI Jeep that was waiting for her at the airstrip outside Boot Hill. She can already feel the relief of this place. Of not having to choose. For the past seven months, necessary safety protocols have grated against her secret yearning to tongue the bumpy capsid of the H7N3 virus. Before that, it was the Rivian Retrovirus. Before that—

She stops herself. She's free now. Here at Kangas Station, she will know relief. The only dangers here will be environmental. Whatever pandemic rages out in the wide world, it won't be able to touch her here. It won't be able to tempt her. She can work, and manage her team, and gaze out across the wide expanse of desert that surrounds her.

She holds out her hand for the stack of keycards. "Appreciate you giving me the chance to run, but it's not going to happen. I can't imagine anywhere I'd rather be."

Kinsey's running hard and fast. Down the hall, around the corner, her heels falling hard on the sand-strewn linoleum. She stops at the airlock door, panicked, then remembers the pile of keycards in the canteen. Doubling back to get them feels risky, but it's worth it—she finds all six of them there, stacked on the scarred coffee table, and she takes them all. Then she books it for the airlock, getting there just as the voices in the residential corridor start to get louder.

She holds the entire handful of keycards up to the reader until it blinks green and that's it. She's out. She slams the heavy door behind her, sealing herself out of the research station.

It's pitch-dark in the airlock. No light, no windows. She leans against the closed interior door. The sound of her own breathing is too loud so she goes still, holds her breath even though it makes her dizzy. She waits to see if she can hear anyone pursuing her. There are quick footfalls from inside the station, the patter of two people on each other's heels.

When she can't hold her breath anymore, Kinsey eases herself away from the door. She stumbles forward, her hands stretched out in front of her, feeling her way toward the squat shelving unit on pure instinct. There's a junky flashlight on one of those shelves, a hefty one with four corroded batteries in it. That flashlight will give her enough light to find the keys to the Jeep. The Jeep will get her out of here.

A silent sob rips out of her as her hands find purchase on the dusty corner of the shelves. Squatting, shaking with unspent adrenaline, she feels her way from shelf to shelf, pushing her hands into the gaps to feel for what's on each one. Past the rustling fabric of Saskia's discarded windbreaker, behind a stack of ancient roadmaps, next to the heavy plastic of a charging walkie-talkie that no one will ever use again—she finally closes her fingers around cool, smooth metal.

The flashlight comes to life in her hands, the white beam cutting away the darkness inside the airlock. She aims it at the wall above the shelves, squints at the glaring white-painted pegboard until her eyes adjust and she can see the keys to the Jeep hanging on their hook. The metal key-edge digs a promise of escape into her palm.

From here it's just a few meters to the exterior door. To the Jeep. To freedom and civilization and certain safety. She turns to run for the exterior door.

She freezes.

She is not alone in the airlock.

The flashlight beam illuminates a face. It stares down from the wall just above the door. As Kinsey watches, paralyzed, a forked tongue emerges to taste the air. To taste her breath and her sweat and her fear.

The face turns to follow the taste of her.

"Kinsey," Domino's voice rasps from somewhere behind the just-parted lips. "Where are you going?"

Kinsey doesn't have time to run. Behind her, she can hear footsteps pattering past the interior door again. She knows it's a matter of minutes before that door opens. In front of her, Domino climbs down the wall, their fingers spread wide to grip the stamped vinyl. A small shower of sand rains down every time they move.

"How did you get out?" Kinsey whispers.

"Nkrumah let me out. She let Saskia out, too. I'm sure they're on their way."

"Let me go," Kinsey pleads. "Please. Just let me leave."

"Where are you going to go?" Domino asks. Another few inches and they'll be blocking the door entirely. Kinsey tries to get a good look at them, but the flashlight flickers and dims. She smacks it hard with her palm. It responds by flickering again. "You love it here," Domino presses. "Why would you leave?"

"To warn people. The world has to know what's coming," she says. "They have to know that you're going to kill them all."

Domino climbs down the wall a little farther, skirting the edges of the flashlight beam. Kinsey can make out only a few details of their body—a ripple of bronze flesh, a long multi-jointed leg splaying out into the shadows. Their contours seem ill-defined, changeable. Shifting. "You don't have to do that," they say. "They'll find out on their own. Everyone dies someday, Kinsey, and hardly anybody gets a warning about it before it happens."

She shakes her head. "Please."

"I don't understand." The barest hint of frustration enters Domino's voice. They shimmy down the wall more, reach out to grasp the doorframe with long, flat fingers. "There's nowhere you love more than this. There's nobody you want more than me. Tell me what you want and I'll give it to you. This doesn't have to be hard."

The doorknob behind Kinsey rattles.

"Give us a minute," Domino calls. "You'll let them in, won't you, Kinsey?"

Kinsey forces herself to look away from Domino. The stack of keycards digs into the soft meat of her fingers—she grips them until they creak, terrified of dropping them before she has a chance to unlock the exterior door. She whips the flashlight from corner to corner, looking for something she can use. The flickering beam falls on abandoned clothes and boots, notebooks and detritus, none of it heavy or sharp or useful at all.

"I'm not letting you leave," Domino says behind her. "Not until you tell me why you don't want to stay. And don't say it's to warn people. That's a lie, and we both know it."

Kinsey turns back to them, and this time, she points the flashlight beam directly onto them.

The light illuminates the fullness of what they've become. It's a perfect, massive facsimile of the lichen's microscopic structure. Arms and legs frill around a wide net of body parts, lips and labia and nipples and ears all strung together across a sticky web of flesh. Lacelike fingers and toes tassel out to stick the creature to the wall. Grains of sand and pearly beads of moisture collect at the places where the long strands of skin intersect. Kinsey can't tell if the liquid is sweat or tears or plasma or pure slick pleasure. The creature's musk fills the airlock, more invasive and inescapable with every second, and Kinsey understands what it tried to tell her when it was pretending to be Domino. She can taste it on the air, just as it swore it could taste her. She can taste its desire. Her tongue curls inside her mouth, seeking more even as she desperately searches for a means of escape.

The creature has spread itself across the door, and it watches Kinsey, waiting patiently for her reply. The doorknob rattles again. "One more minute," Domino calls.

"Why?!" The voice on the other side of the door is Saskia's, and it's impatient.

"Go let them in," Domino murmurs. "They want you. I want you."

"But I don't want this," Kinsey hisses.

"Bullshit." It draws itself inward even further, consolidating the matrix of flesh into a tighter mesh. "Of course you want me. I can feel it, Kinsey. And—and I saw you," they add.

Kinsey shakes her head. "Saw—?"

The head that wears Domino's face rotates. It stretches toward her, sand hissing off it in streams. "I saw the way you looked at me when you brought me inside. I saw the way you blushed when I looked back at you. I heard you fucking yourself, over and over again, while I was making my home inside your colleagues. I felt the way you responded when I touched you. Kinsey, come on," it pleads. "Stop playing this game."

She wets her lips. "I don't want this," she says softly. The thing between her and the door opens its mouth, but she cuts it off. "No, don't—don't interrupt. I'm telling you the truth, and I want you to tell the others, too. This—all of this," she adds, gesturing behind her to include the creature with Mads's body, the thing that's shaped like Nkrumah, the remains of Jacques's corpse. "I don't want it."

"But—"

"I want *you*," she says, and saying it feels like ripping a fishhook out of the root of her own tongue. "I want you as you are. I don't want this, this, this—" She can't find a word for it, settles for simply holding out a hand toward the mess that wears her dead colleagues' tongues and cocks and cunts like jewelry. "I know you're trying your hardest to be what I want. I know you think I'm some kind of puzzle to be solved. But I'm not that. I don't want tricks and surprises and new shapes. I don't want to feel like I'm fucking someone else!" She's yelling now, her eyes burning with angry tears. She's never fought with a lover before. It's awful and it's wonderful, the truth carving its way free of her on a wave of strange hot fury. "I don't want Saskia or Domino or Mads! I've never wanted them!"

"Kinsey," the thing on the wall ventures, but Kinsey's momentum is too powerful and she cuts it off again.

"If I wanted them, I would have fucked them! You stupid fucking *thing*!" She swings at it with the flashlight, misses. "I've never fucked myself thinking about them, I've never lost sleep over them, why would you think I *want* them when I only want *you*!" She swings again, catches a strand of flesh with the very end of the flashlight. There's a snag and a snap and the creature releases a strained cry of pain. "You think you saw me? You don't know what you saw! I looked at you and felt something real, and I knew we couldn't be together, I knew you couldn't ever want me back, and I was okay with it! I was used to it! But this?" She lets out a laugh, feels the spill of tears on her cheeks. "This is worse than nothing. You've given me everything *but* what I want. You've made a grotesque fucking joke of what we could have been. I don't want this," she says one last time. "I. Want. To. *Leave*."

SPREAD ME

With that, she swings the flashlight at them again. This time she hits center mass. The heavy metal of the flashlight strikes the dense web of tissue. Domino screams, a piercing shriek like wind whipping through the desert at night, a coyote-howl of pain. Kinsey wrenches her arm back and then swings again, tearing through the network of flesh. No, she realizes—it only seems like flesh. It's a close facsimile, but the fungus can't repair itself fast enough to disguise the spongy give of densely connected hyphae.

She swings the flashlight again and again, pounding the creature in front of her until it hangs in shreds, and it's only when the thing stops screeching that she realizes she's screaming, too.

"I don't want you," Kinsey replies breathlessly. "Not any of you. Not after what you've done." She feels behind her back, groping her way through the mash that's left of Domino until her hand finds the stripe of metal that is the exterior door handle.

"You're making a mistake," a voice says from behind the interior door. "There's nothing for you out there."

She shakes her head, pressing the stack of keycards to the reader until it flashes green. "That's where you're wrong." And with that, she opens the door and flees the station, her feet pounding against the sand as she makes her way to the Jeep, to the desert.

To freedom.

Only half the lights are on in Sweet Ramona's. It's the end of the night. The team has taken over the long, scarred table in the middle of the room. Ramona herself approaches with a tray of shots—something dark and bitter that no one ordered.

"Sounds like things are going well for you kids tonight," she says, raising one tattoo-notched eyebrow at the jar of cash that sits in the middle of the table. It's surrounded by a sea of discarded shot glasses. "This round's on me."

The tray of shots looks like a revolver chamber full of oiled bullets. Everyone on the team takes one, their tongues already flinching away from the idea of whatever Ramona might be inflicting on the group. Kinsey raises her glass in a wobbling hand, and looks around the table.

"Domino. Mads. Nkrumah. Jacques. Saskia. You all decided tonight that you want to stay out here, in this fucking gorgeous awful place, for another six months. Every single one of you is a fool for giving up the opportunity to return to polite society."

At the opposite end of the table, Mads raises their shot back to her. "What about you, Boss?"

Domino goes next. "Will you stay?"

Jacques follows. "Or will you go?"

Saskia raps the bottom of her glass on the table before lifting it. "With us?"

Nkrumah goes last. "Or alone?"

Kinsey raises her hand high overhead. The smell of Ramona's round slaps her hard, bitter and herbal. She grins at her team. Her friends. Her family.

"I'm in it 'til the end."

They drink together, shout expletives at the diesel taste of the liquor, and together, bring their jar of cash to the bar. They can't think of anything that could possibly tear them away from this place.

The night air wraps around Kinsey's bare thighs as she pulls herself up into the Jeep. The wind isn't as bad as it's going to be, but it still twines freezing fingers through Kinsey's hair, tangling it behind her. It sinks through the thin fabric of her shirt, plucks at the skin over her ribs, bites at her throat.

She slides the key into the ignition, presses her bare toes against the grooved plastic of the gas pedal, and takes off into the night, leaving the station and everything in it behind.

She doesn't bother turning the headlights on. After the Jeep has eaten a few miles of dirt road, she eases her foot off the gas. The car rolls to a stop sooner than she would have guessed—the weight of it, she supposes, is more than enough to arrest its momentum. There's no need for the brakes, no need even to take the keys out of the ignition. She leaves the Jeep where it is, idling in the middle of the ribbon of packed dirt that cuts through the sand and connects the station to the main road.

The desert stretches out around her like clean bedsheets stretched across a new mattress. A hundred miles of sand in every direction, a million flowers, a billion insects. There's more life around her than there is inside her. She sifts her bare feet through the sand. She's never done this before—never walked out into the desert without protection on every part of her body, sunscreen and hiking boots and thick wool socks, a hat and sunglasses, everything she could think of to prevent her and this place from truly touching each other.

"You," she whispers, toeing a hole in the sand that she knows leads down into an anthill humming with activity. The tickle of legs on her ankle as the ants respond to the threat of her presence, the sting of a bite on the inside of her knee. She keeps walking, feels a rock embed itself into the bottom of her foot. "You," she says again.

There are more stars in the sky here than anywhere else on earth. She doesn't know if that's true, but she's always thought it. A coyote lets out a series of demonic yips in the distance and she understands—she also wants to scream, to cry, to rip the sky into confetti with the sounds that can emerge from her throat.

"I can't believe I said all that," she says, her voice coming out hoarse. She steps over a shadow that might be a cactus and might be a rock and might be nothing at all. The wind picks up, whistling the sand into eddies all around her. "I can't believe I yelled like that. I'm sorry."

There's a rustling behind her. She looks over her shoulder and sees nothing. Not a figure, not movement. Not the Jeep, either—it's out of sight, which she knows means she'll never find it again. Getting lost in the desert is as easy as blinking, as easy as getting distracted. As easy as walking a few paces in the wrong direction.

"I meant it, though," she says, feeling her way forward. Something scuttles out of her way. "I meant everything I said. I didn't want any of what you did." There's a space in front of her, a clear patch where maybe something got ripped out of the earth and blew away. She squats and runs her hands across it, shifting sand to one side. "I didn't want the theatre. I didn't want the games. Do you understand?" The wind sweeps across the desert toward her, making her shiver. "I don't want you to make a body for me. I don't want you to steal someone else's cock and fuck me with it. I don't want you wet and moaning, I don't want you soft and panting—I don't want that."

She stands to look down at the dark patch of black sand she's unearthed. It shouldn't have been this easy to dig down to, not with her bare hands, not this fast. It's almost as though the desert peeled itself back for her.

She's looking down at the cryptobiotic crust—the layer of life under the desert, the home of everything that moves beneath the sand and keeps the soil where it belongs. The cryptobiotic crust, which is, in this place, infected. Kinsey looks at it and she knows it's sick, because she feels heat rising in her like the sun coming up over the rocks. Need pulses in her, between her legs and up her belly and in her throat.

She pulls her shirt and underwear off in a rush, throwing them into the darkness for the elements to tear to pieces. No one will ever find them. Not out here.

Kinsey steps forward gingerly, aware that she's destroying life with every step. Gooseflesh rises across her shoulders.

The wind teases her taut nipples, curls its way between her legs, tugs her forward.

She sinks to her knees between the piles of sand she's cleared away. A shiver overtakes her as her skin comes into contact with the viral lichen that lives beneath the desert soil.

"I only want you," she says. "I want you as you are. I want you to be with me. But not the way humans are with each other. We only know how to fuck things or kill things, or fuck things until we've killed them, or kill things until it feels like fucking them." She eases herself onto her stomach and presses her mouth against the sand, letting it coat her tongue with grit and salt. "I want you in more ways than that. Better ways. I want you inside me. I want you as you are."

The living thing beneath the desert surface hears her. It winds the virus around her ankles, her wrists, her throat. It reaches fingers of fungal hyphae into her mouth, traces the veins of her tongue. It hums through the sweet folds of her vocal cords to draw a scream out of her, the kind of ecstatic sound she's longed to make for as long as she can remember. She digs her fingers into the sand, curls her toes into the minute paths carved by wind and scant water, sings a song of brutal sun and static storms and high screaming winds.

The lichen rises up out of the earth to kiss the tenderest, pinkest parts of her, the places where she's most alive. It makes her feel the blistering pink of the sunset over the dunes, the high-noon screech of a dying thing's thirst. It stretches her wide and wet, feels the velvet of her deepest pleasure, pushes her open until her tendons creak with strain. Finally, when she can't bear it anymore, when she cries out to the darkness in agony and ecstasy and perfect sweet becoming—finally, at last, the virus takes her, sinking itself into her cells all the way to the hilt.

And it understands, as it draws her into spun filaments of ecstasy, that she really did mean everything she said. She wants it just as it is: perfect, and hungry, and alive.

She takes it all.

ACKNOWLEDGMENTS

It is often tempting—and occasionally necessary—to create for oneself a desert in which to hide. The sticky humidity of becoming known to loved ones can become overwhelming, and sometimes the danger of being perceived by our enemies threatens to drown us. Loneliness is arid. It can be a relief to dehydrate for a while, safe and secure in the vast dry stretch of an unobserved existence.

But even in those isolated seasons of dreadful relief, there is no such thing, for any of us, as *alone*. The desert teems with life, above and below the surface of the sand. What lives there is hardy, resourceful, thrifty, and canny. The desert is not barren; it's lush with survivors. When we take ourselves off to the desert to be alone, we find ourselves surrounded by those who know how to endure.

Thank you to all who have been, for months and years and decades, fighting the tides that threaten to drown those of us who stand closest to the shoreline. Thank you to all those who have had to take themselves into the desert in order to avoid the encroaching undertow of fear, hatred, and oppression; thank you to those who have returned from that desert, determined to fight. Thank you to those who organize networks of aid to protect those who are standing with their feet in the water, and those who are standing on high dunes.

Thank you to my loved ones, who are the reason I have survived both the desert and the sea.

Thank you to everyone, everywhere, who shares our stories. Thank you to those who create, promote, and protect art. Including this book, which has been guarded by brilliant, tireless advocates throughout the creative process.

To the agent, early readers, editors (both of you), copyeditor, sales and marketing teams, art director, cover artist, interior designer, production team, interns, publicists, book bloggers, critics who love the book, critics who think the book is just okay, critics who don't care for the book, critics who didn't read the book, booksellers, librarians, readers, and all my fellow writers, published and unpublished—all of you growing, all of you searching, all of you forever alive:

Thank you for loving art. Thank you for sticking your hands deep into the sand at the shoreline and the sand in the desert, thank you for grabbing great fistfuls of muck and life, thank you for pressing your palms to your face and inhaling the luxurious stink of existence. Keep digging deep. Art loves you back, especially when you're not afraid to meet it at its depths.

And to you who are looking out at the water and out at the desert and trying to decide if it's even worth it to try to survive one or the other: Thank you for being with me in this book. You are never alone. You are being thought of. You are being written for, sung for, painted for, danced for, fought for. Even if it's happening in places where you can't see it—even if you are swimming for your life or enduring the relentless sun, and all you can focus on is survival. Even then. We are here, with our hands deep in the earth, loving you.

If you so need, help is available at the Trans Lifeline (1-877-565-8860);

ACKNOWLEDGMENTS

As well as twenty-four hours a day via The Trevor Project (1-866-488-7386 or by texting START to 678-678);

And from the Suicide & Crisis Lifeline (dial 988) at any time.

ABOUT THE AUTHOR

Kate Dollarhyde 2023

Sarah Gailey is a Hugo Award–winning and bestselling author of speculative fiction, short stories, and essays. Their nonfiction has been published by dozens of venues internationally. Their fiction has been published in more than seven different languages. Their work includes their bestselling adult novel debut, *Magic for Liars; The Echo Wife; Just Like Home;* and their original comic book series with BOOM! Studios, *Know Your Station*. You can find links to their work at sarahgailey.com.